Sports Illustrated KIDS
GRAPHIC NOVELS

STONE ARCH BOOKS
a capstone imprint

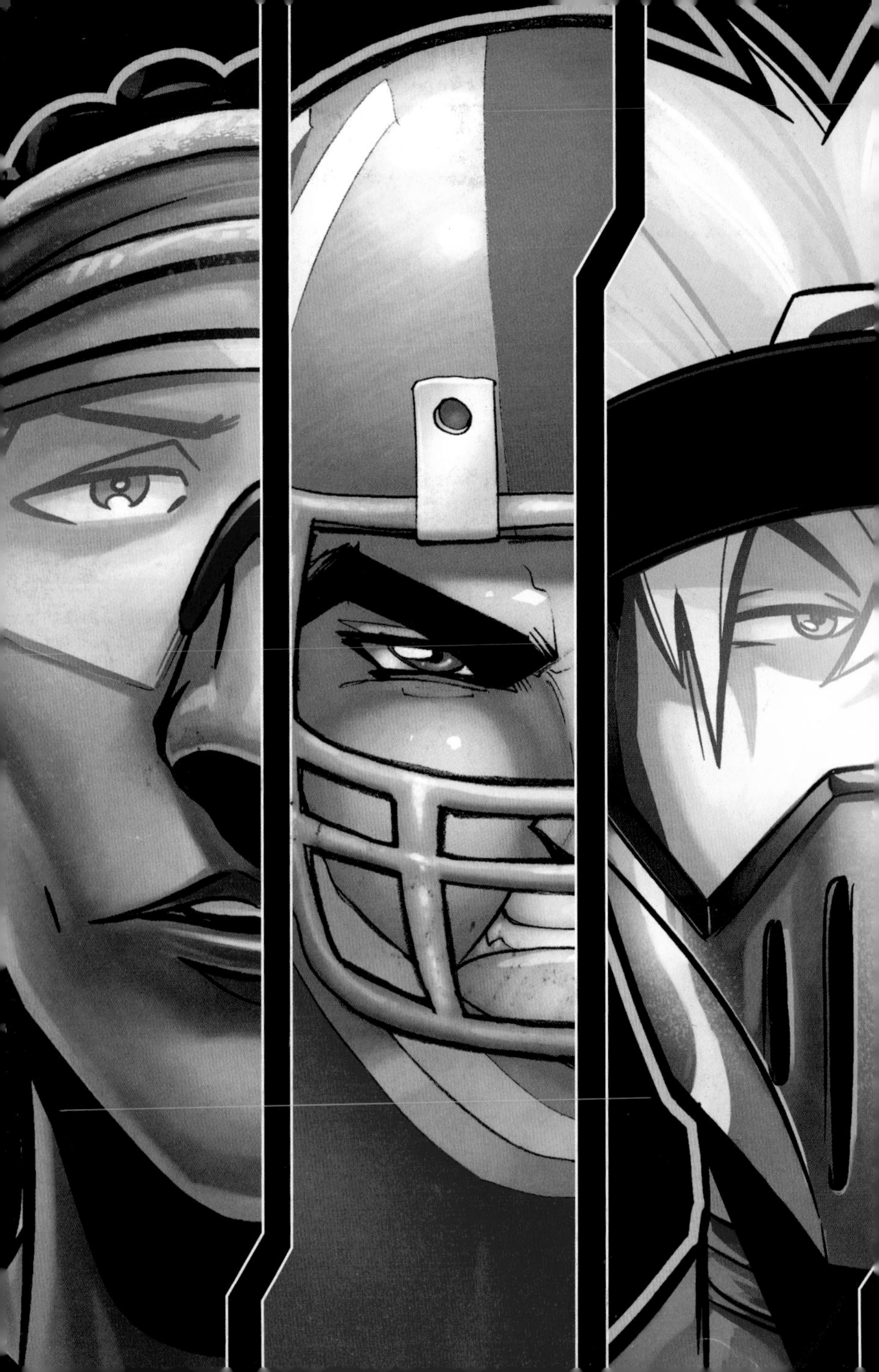

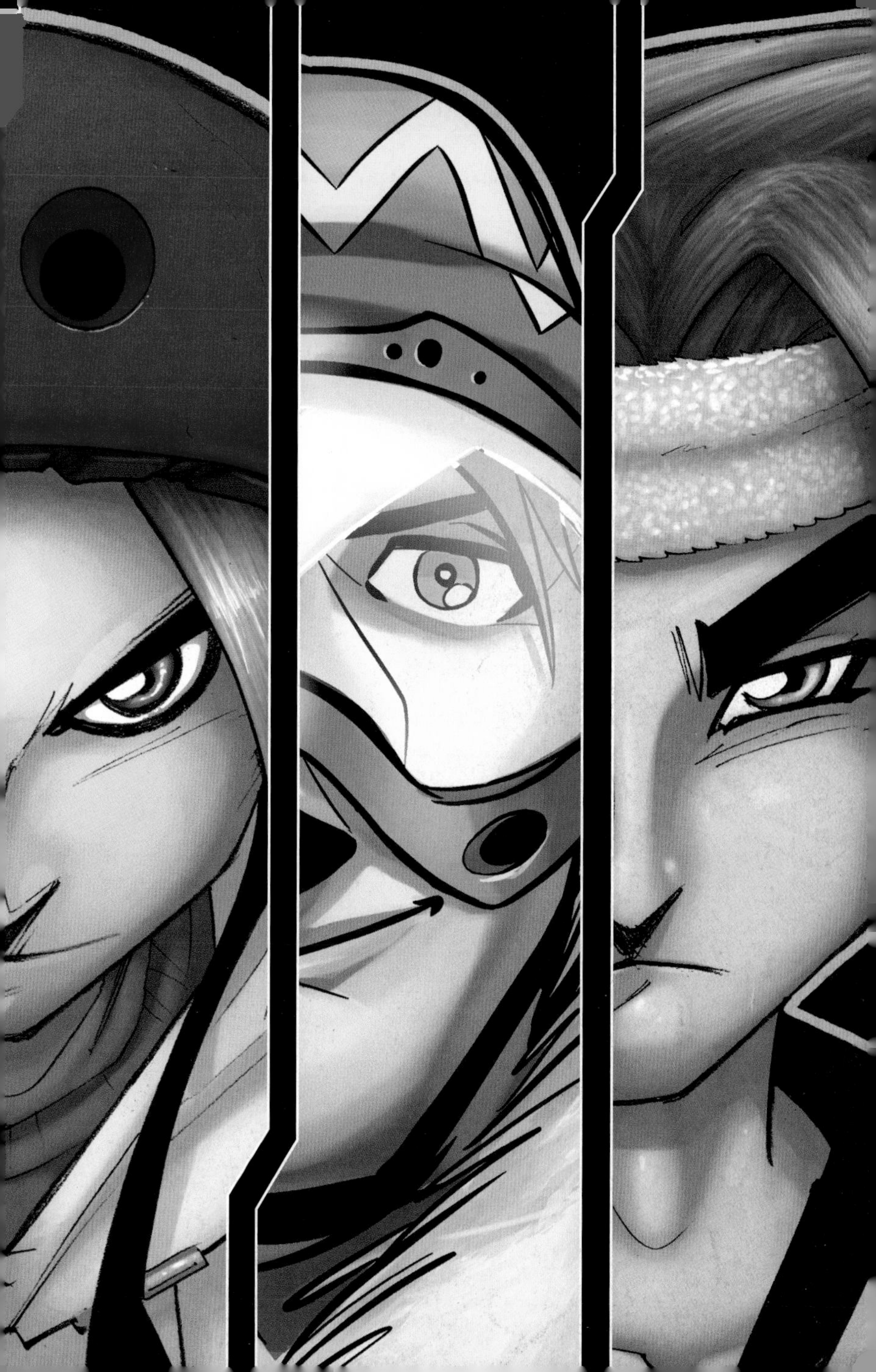

UP NEXT ›››

on Sports Illustrated KIDS

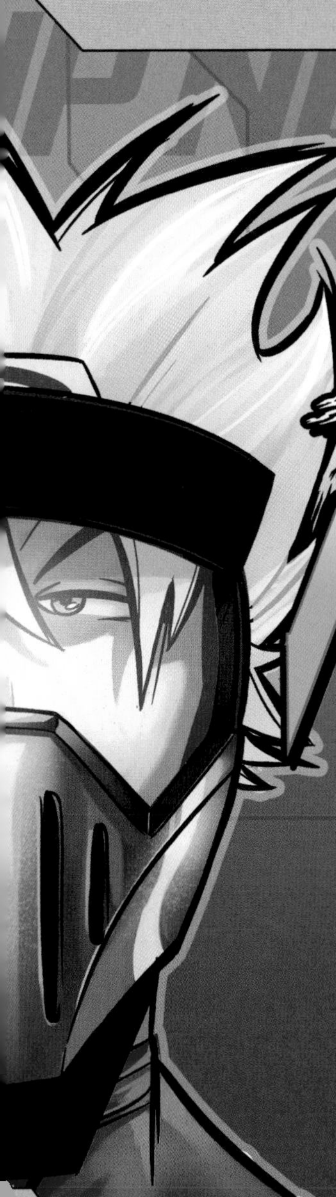

:02 SPORTS ZONE SPECIAL REPORT

:04 FEATURE PRESENTATION:

PAINTBALL PUNK

FOLLOWED BY:

:50 SPORTS ZONE POSTGAME RECAP

:51 SPORTS ZONE POSTGAME EXTRA

:52 SI KIDS INFO CENTER

RIOT REMAIN UNDEFEATED AS THEY ROLL INTO STATE FINALS SIK TICKER

SPORTS ZONE

ECIAL REPORT

NT
BALL

O
ING

L

L

L
LL

WOLVES TOP TEAMMATE REFUSES TO PLAY NICE

CHESTER COYOTE

STATS:
POSITION: SCOUT
AGE: 14
TEAM: WOLVES

BIO: Chester Coyote doesn't play well with others. It's not that he's a bad guy — he just doesn't quite get the whole "teamwork" thing. He likes to hang out with his friends, and he loves playing paintball . . . just not at the same time. If he can't figure out a way to run with the pack against the Riot, this lone wolf will get picked off — and fast.

Sports Illustrated KIDS

UP NEXT: PAINTBALL PUNK

BLZ vs BRS
3-1
TGR vs ROR
33-32
EAG vs BAN
14-7
SPA vs WLD
4-3
BAN vs ROR
21-15
RZR vs LIG
4-3
BLZ vs BRS
3-1
TGR vs ROR

CORA RAMIREZ

TEAM: WOLVES   **AGE:** 14
POSITION: POINT

BIO: Cora is the Wolves' team captain and strategist. Her tactical skills are often the difference between victory and defeat for the Wolves. In fact, most of their biggest wins have resulted from her strategies.

PETER ECCLESTON

TEAM: WOLVES   **POSITION:** MARKSMAN   **AGE:** 15
BIO: Peter is a professional in the making. He's calm under pressure, an excellent sharpshooter, and he always plays well with others.

ECCLESTON

JACK BOWSER

TEAM: WOLVES   **POSITION:** ANCHOR   **AGE:** 14
BIO: Jack's much stronger than the average 14-year-old. As the team's anchor, he lays down cover fire and guards the rear.

BOWSER

THE RIOT

AGES: 13-15
BIO: The Riot are trained by S.W.A.T., an elite police unit. The team hasn't lost a single paintball match in two years.

the RIOT

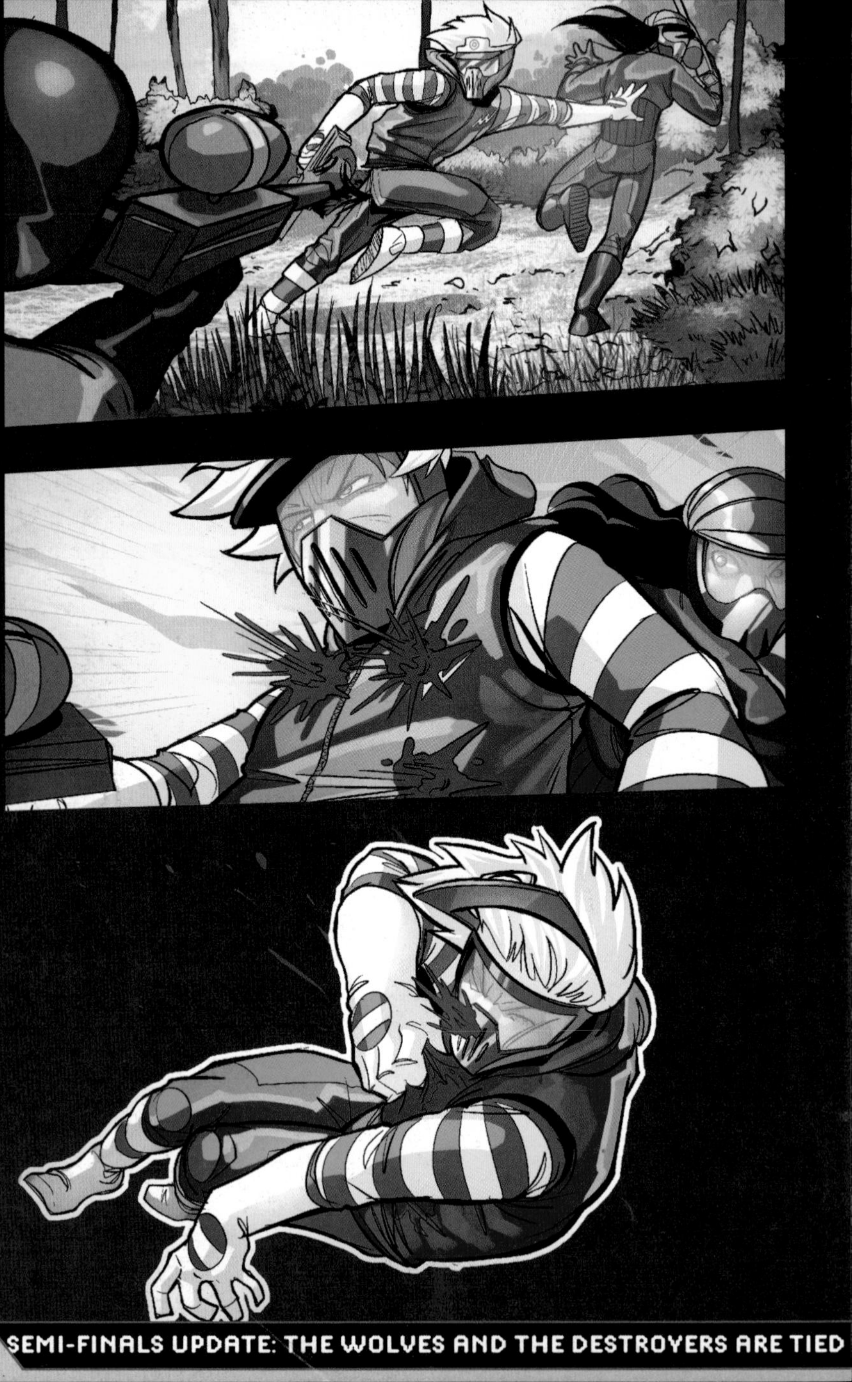
SEMI-FINALS UPDATE: THE WOLVES AND THE DESTROYERS ARE TIED

Sports Illustrated **KIDS**

PRESENTS

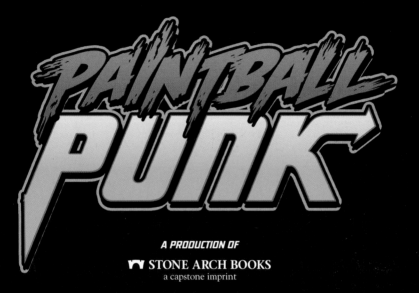

A PRODUCTION OF

STONE ARCH BOOKS
a capstone imprint

written by **Sean Tulien**
illustrated by **Aburtov**
inked by **Andres Esparza**
colored by **Fares Maese**

designed and directed by **Bob Lentz**
creative direction by **Heather Kindseth**
editorial direction by **Michael Dahl**

Sports Illustrated KIDS *Paintball Punk* is published by Stone Arch Books,
151 Good Counsel Drive, P.O. Box 669, Mankato, Minnesota 56002.
www.capstonepub.com

Copyright © 2011 by Stone Arch Books, a Capstone imprint.

Summary: Chester Coyote is a talented paintball player. Unfortunately, he
would rather be a lone wolf than run with the pack. His team, the Wolves,
is in the state paintball finals, but he isn't seeing eye-to-eye with his best
friend, Cora Ramirez, the team's captain. Chester won't follow her orders,
and his class-clown personality is turning the rest of the pack against
him. If Chester doesn't decide to play well with others, he'll lose his
friends — as well as the paintball championship.

Cataloging-in-Publication Data is available at the Library of Congress
website.

ISBN: 978-1-4342-2219-0 (library binding)
ISBN: 978-1-4342-2788-1 (paperback)

Printed in the United States of America in Stevens Point, Wisconsin.
012011   006049R

ATCH EACH — THIRD AND FINAL MATCH IS IN PROGRESS . . **SIK** *TICKER*

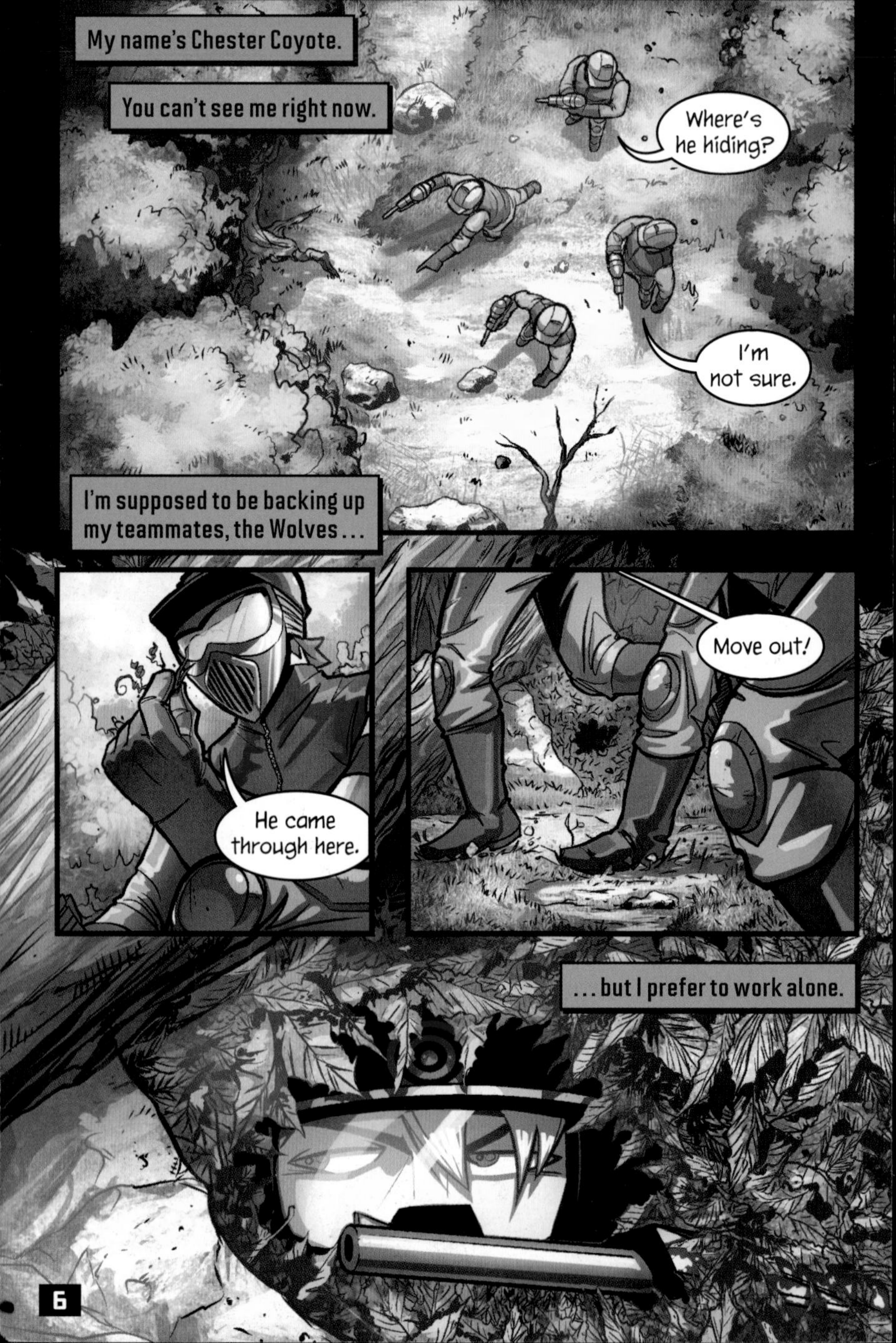
My name's Chester Coyote.
You can't see me right now.
Where's he hiding?
I'm not sure.
I'm supposed to be backing up my teammates, the Wolves . . .
He came through here.
Move out!
. . . but I prefer to work alone.

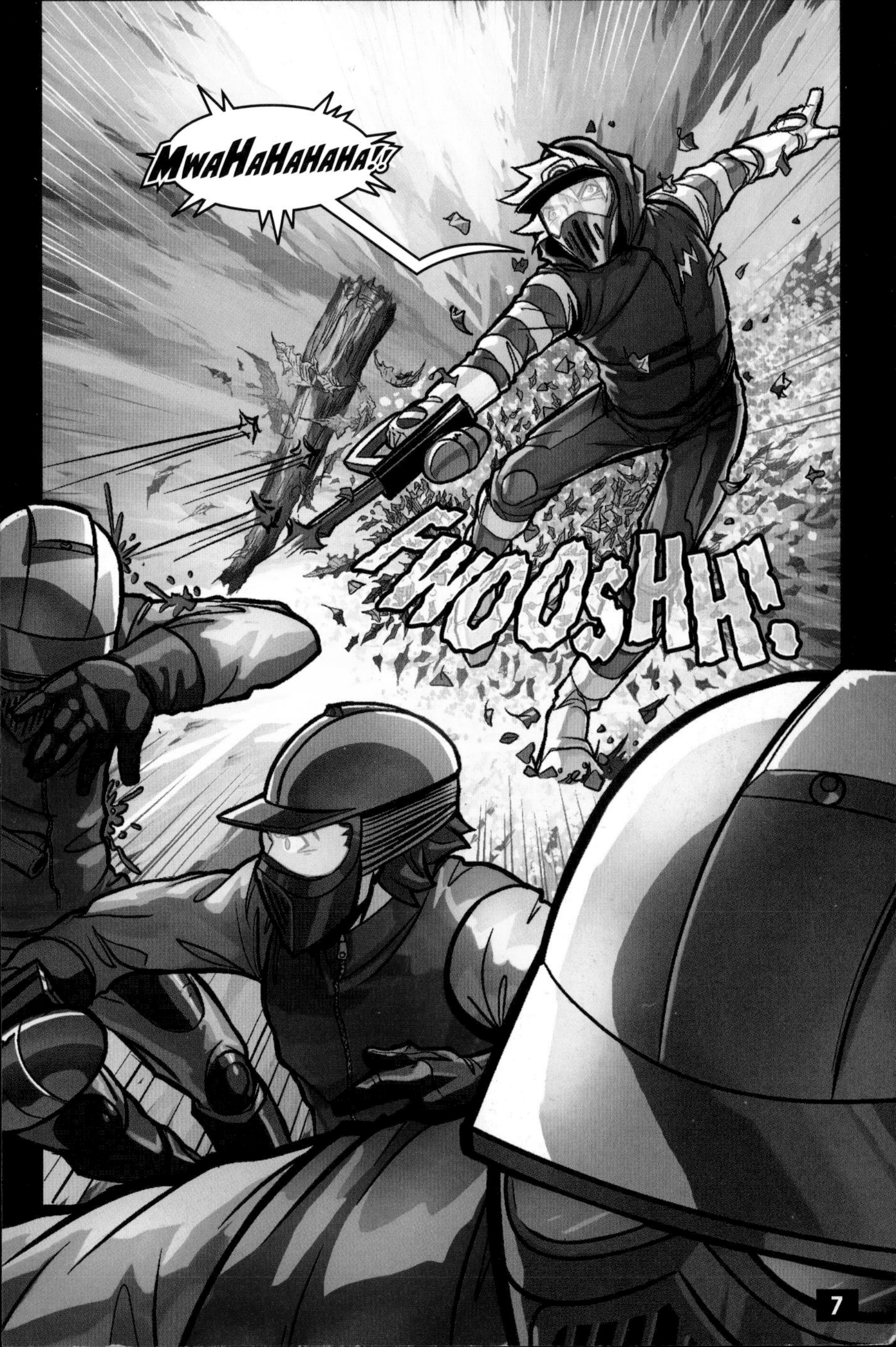
MWAHAHAHAHA!!
FWOOSHH!

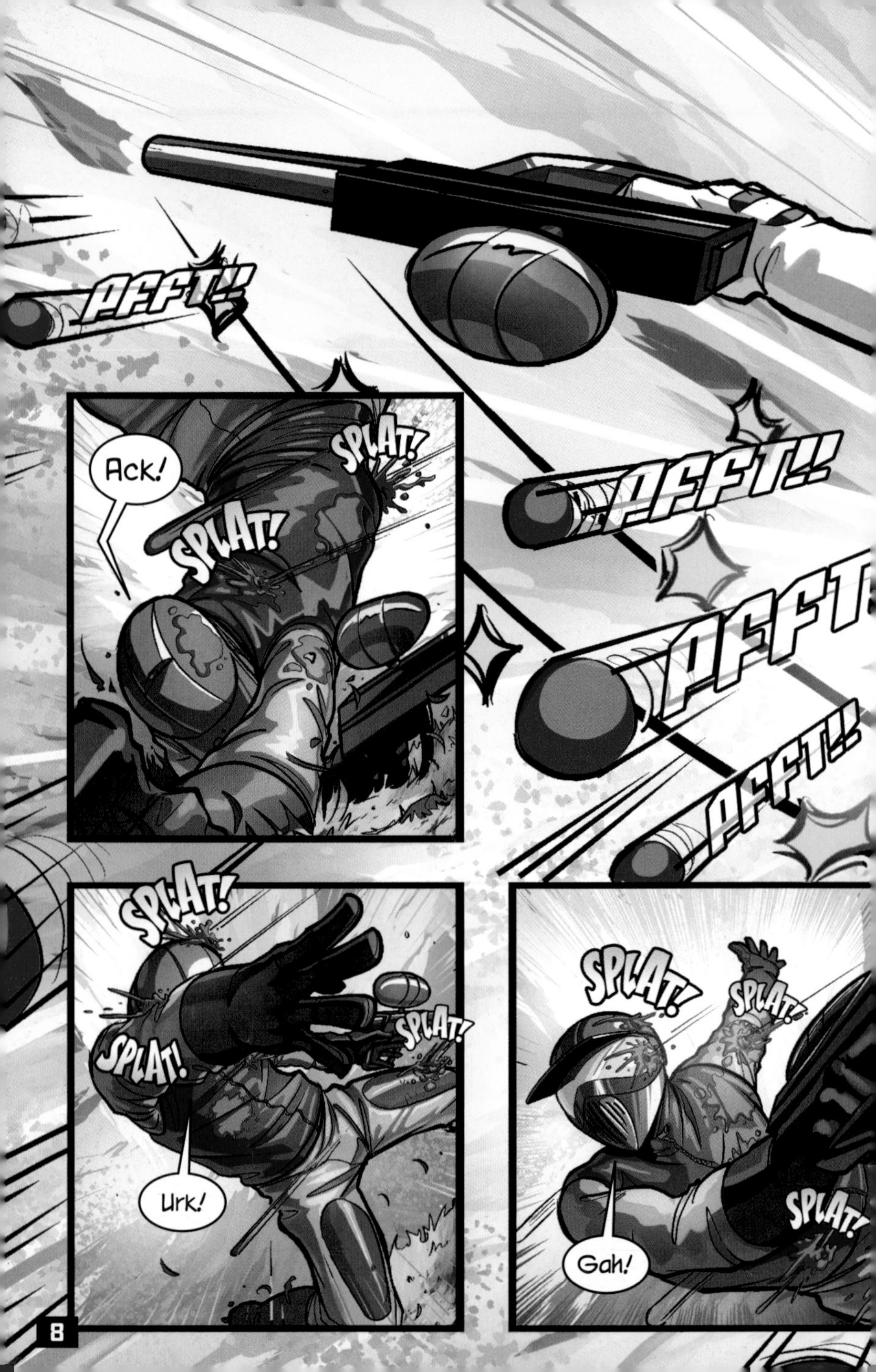
PFFT!!
Ack!
SPLAT!
SPLAT!
PFFT!!
PFFT!
PFFT!!
SPLAT!
SPLAT!
SPLAT!
Urk!
SPLAT!
SPLAT!
SPLAT!
Gah!

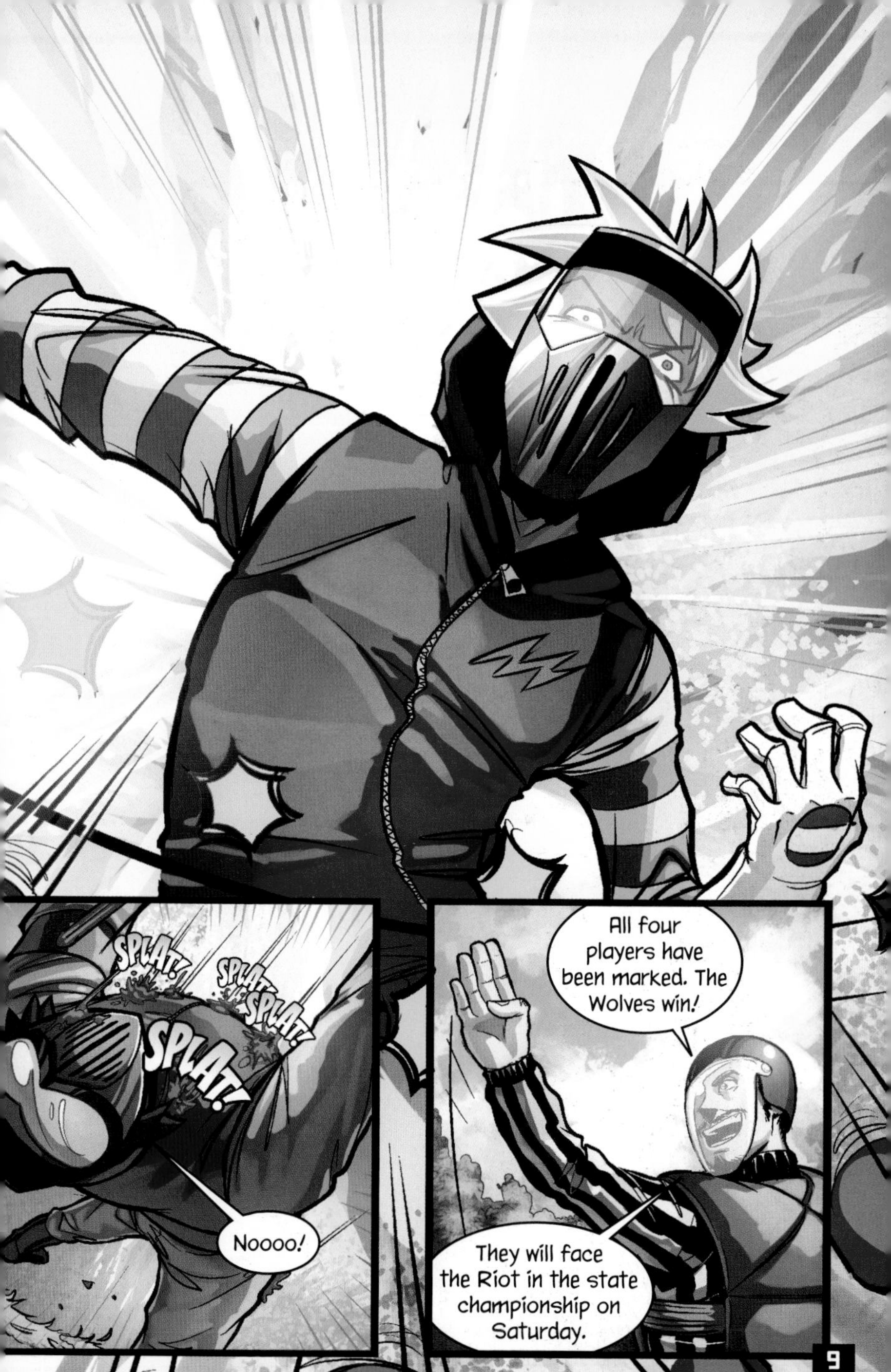
SPLAT!
SPLAT!
SPLAT!
SPLAT!
Noooo!
All four players have been marked. The Wolves win!
They will face the Riot in the state championship on Saturday.

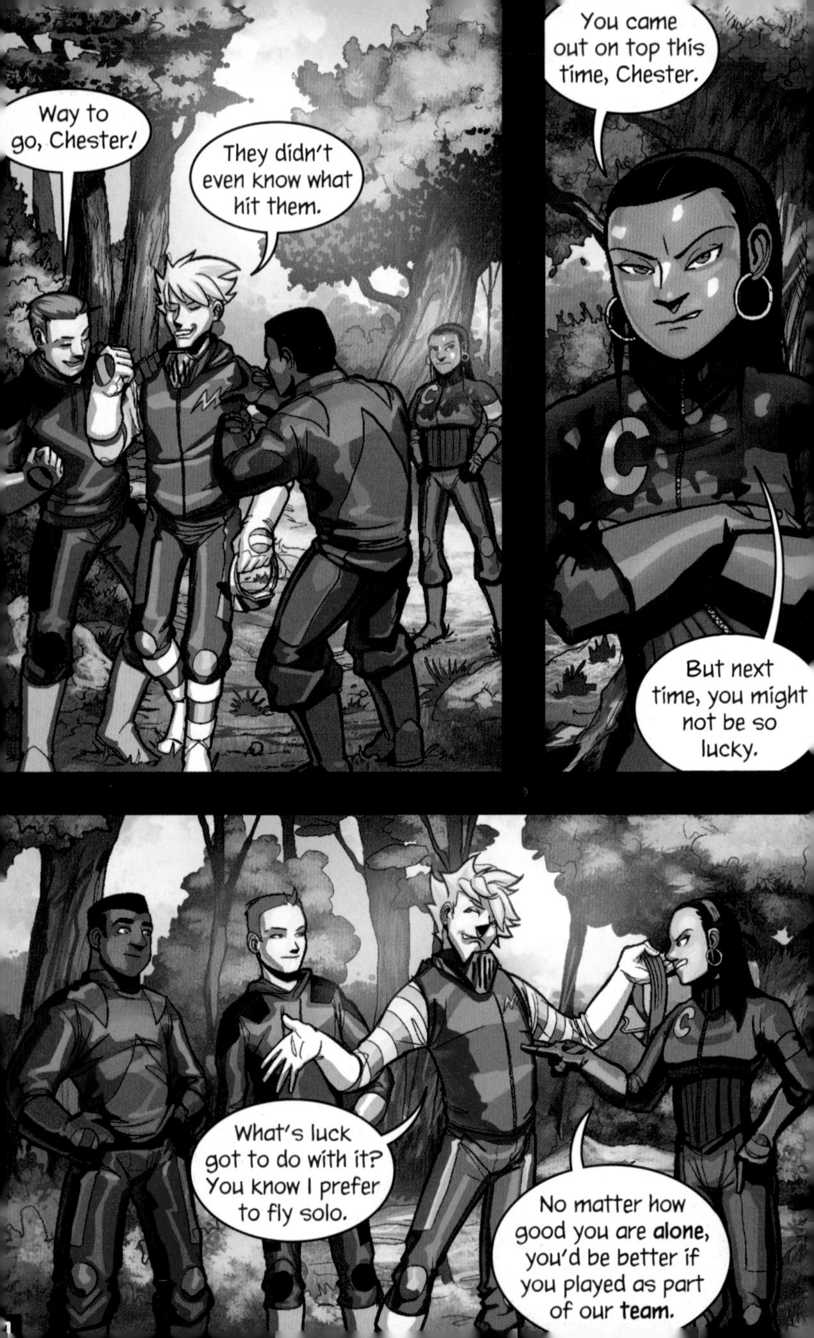
Way to go, Chester!
They didn't even know what hit them.
You came out on top this time, Chester.
But next time, you might not be so lucky.
What's luck got to do with it? You know I prefer to fly solo.
No matter how good you are **alone**, you'd be better if you played as part of our **team**.

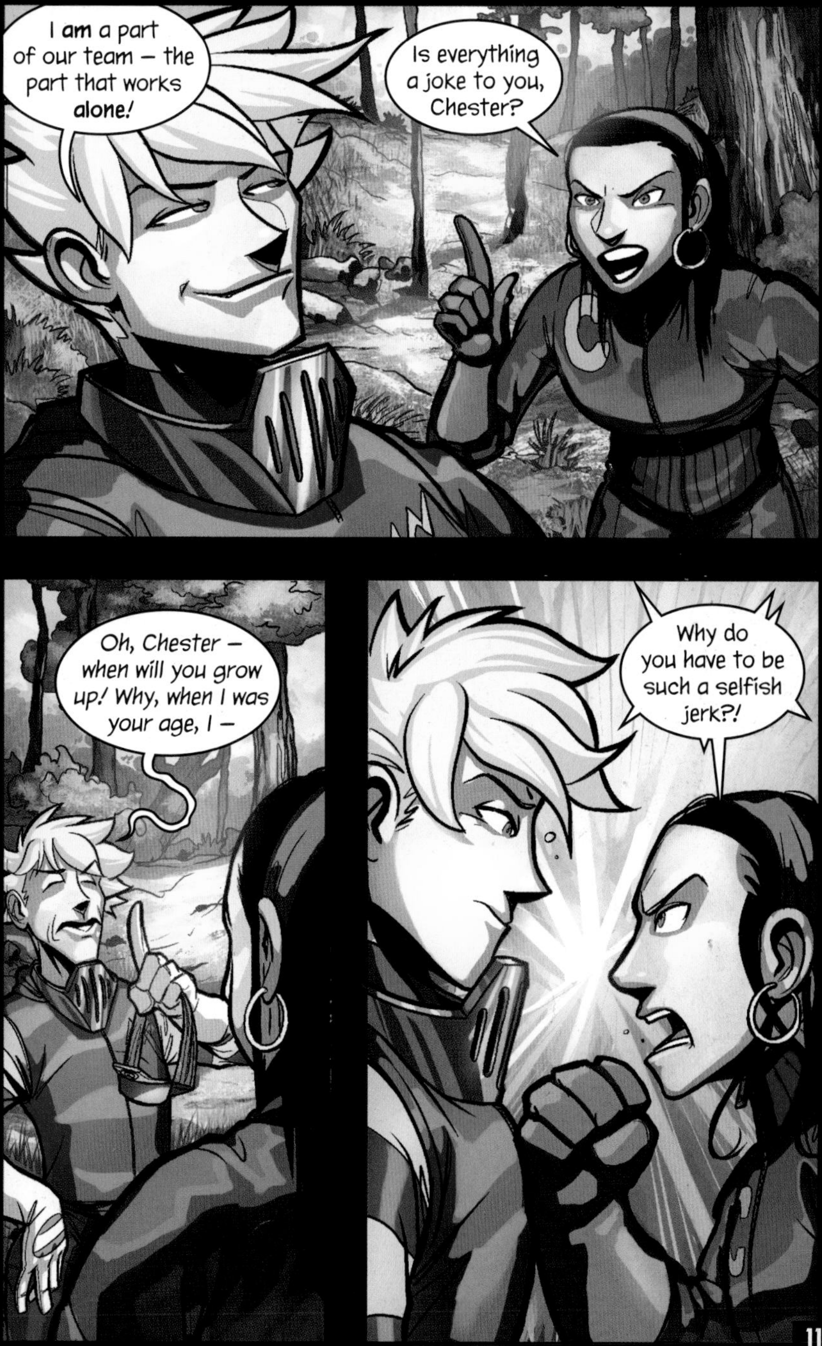

I **am** a part of our team — the part that works **alone**!
Is everything a joke to you, Chester?
Oh, Chester — when will you grow up! Why, when I was your age, I —
Why do you have to be such a selfish jerk?!

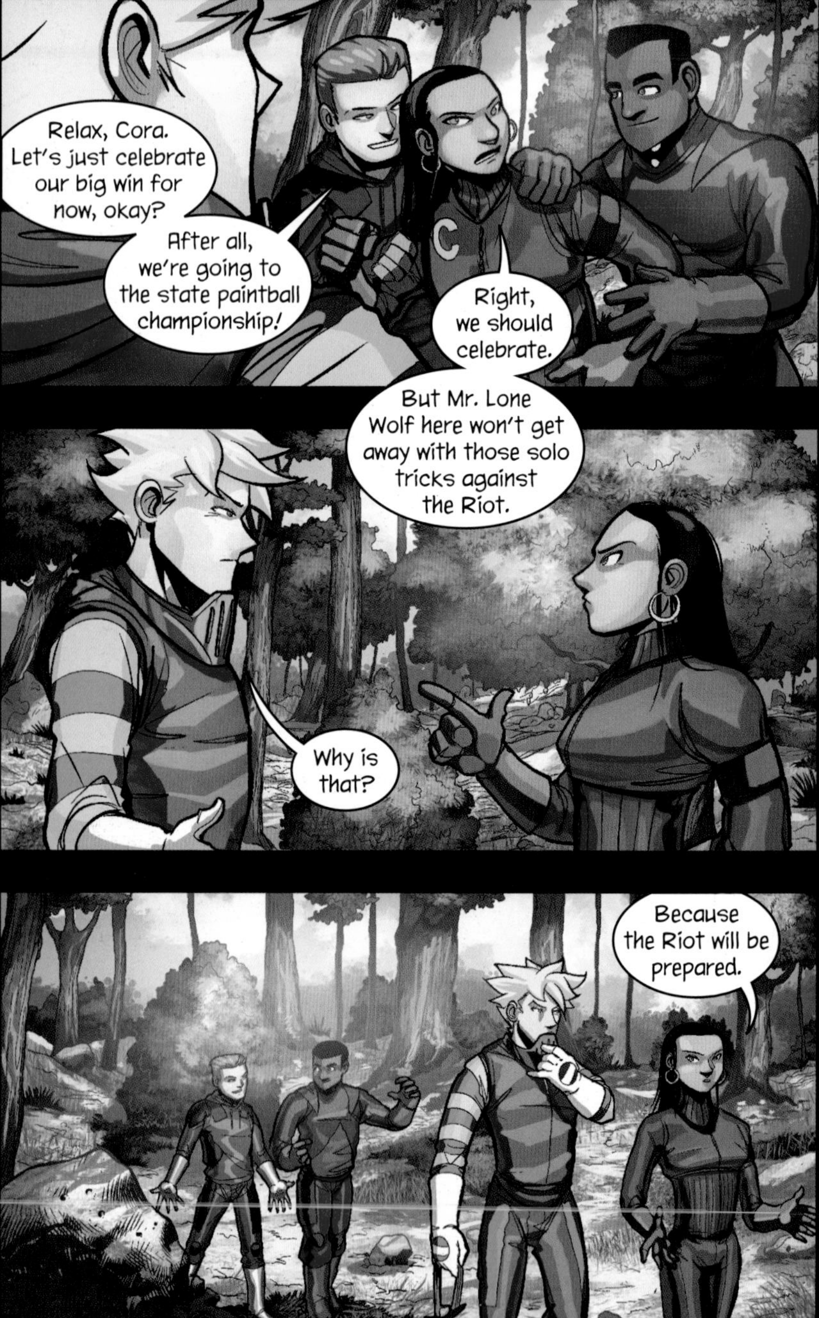
Relax, Cora. Let's just celebrate our big win for now, okay?
After all, we're going to the state paintball championship!
Right, we should celebrate.
But Mr. Lone Wolf here won't get away with those solo tricks against the Riot.
Why is that?
Because the Riot will be prepared.

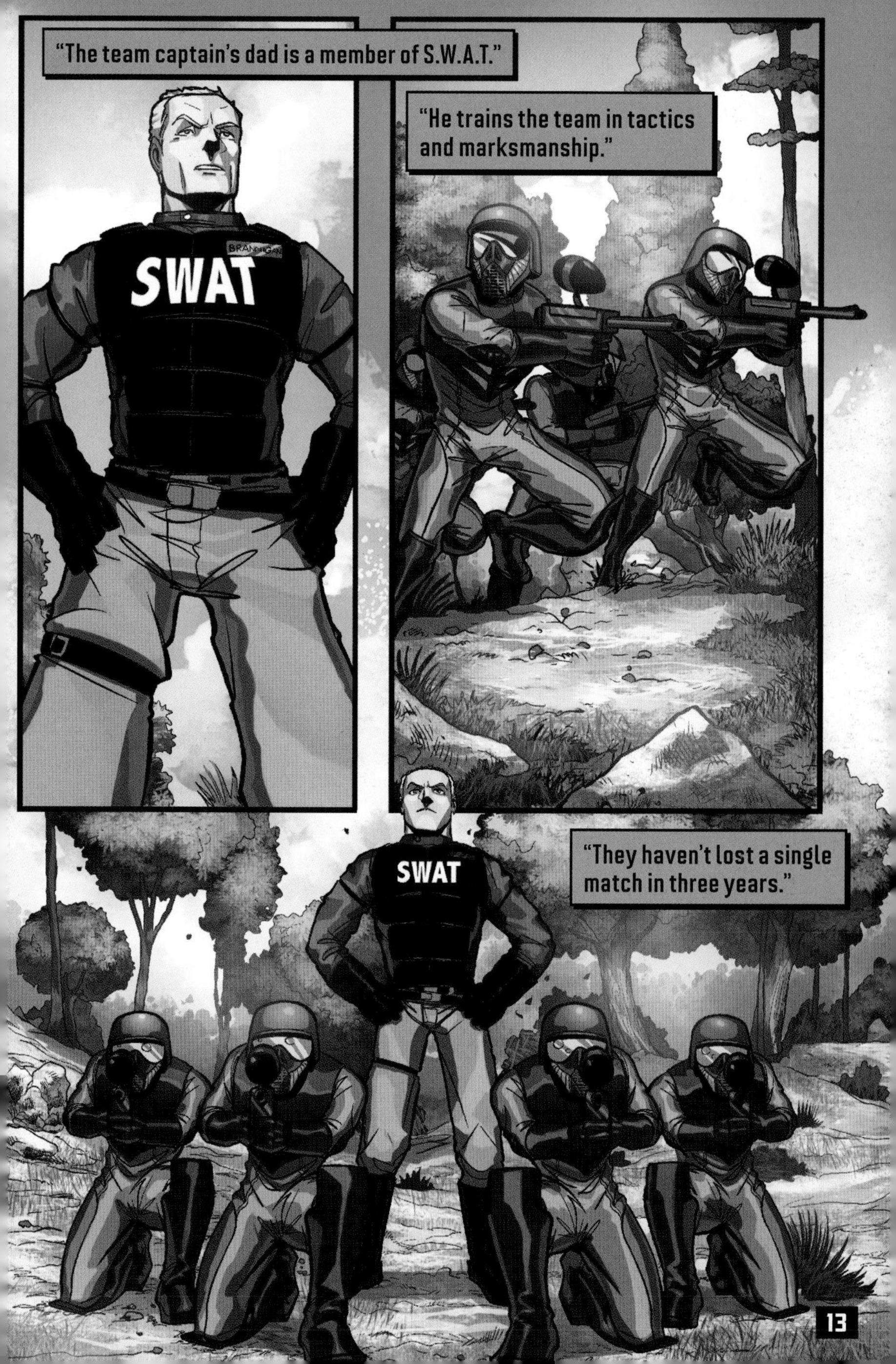
"The team captain's dad is a member of S.W.A.T."
SWAT
"He trains the team in tactics and marksmanship."
SWAT
"They haven't lost a single match in three years."

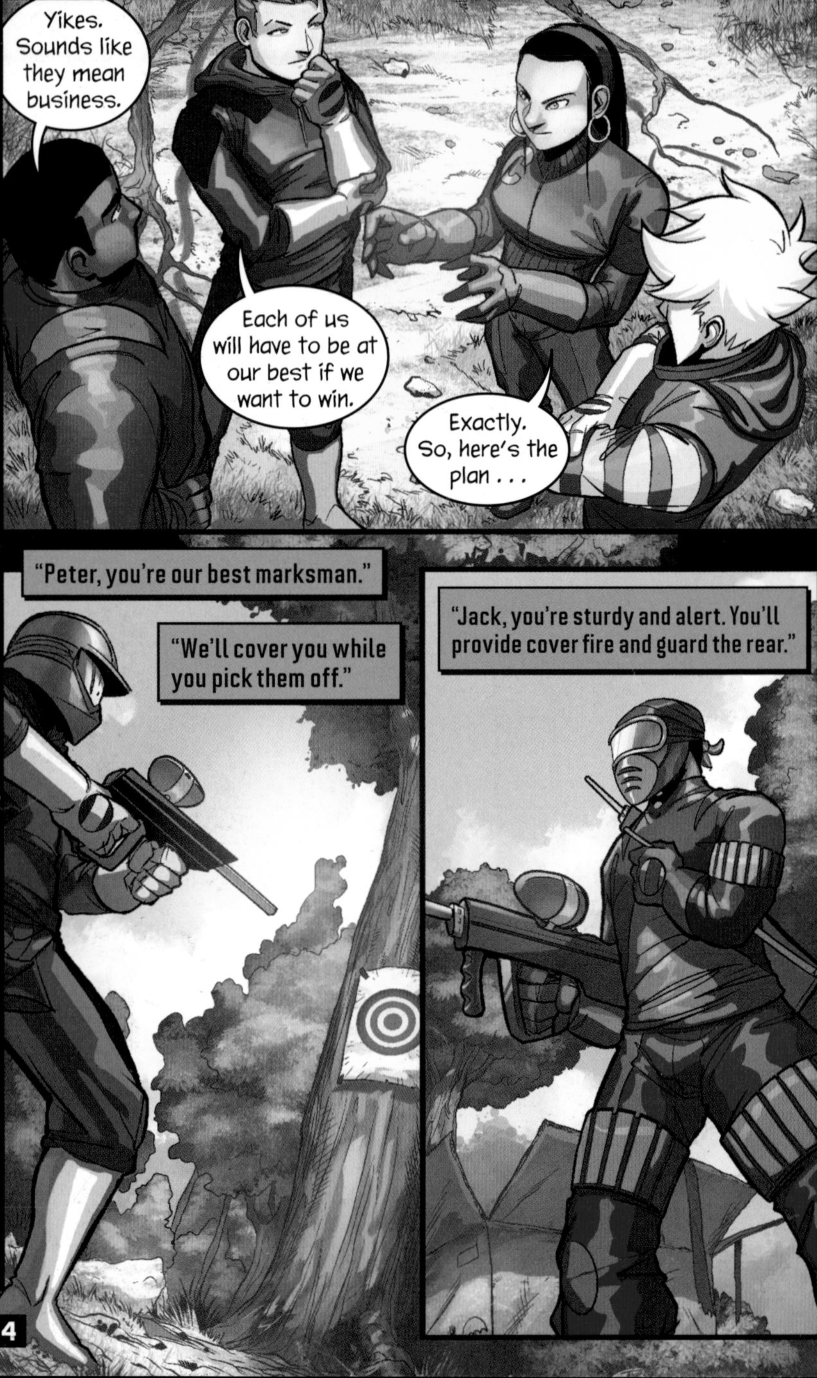
Yikes. Sounds like they mean business.
Each of us will have to be at our best if we want to win.
Exactly. So, here's the plan . . .
"Peter, you're our best marksman."
"We'll cover you while you pick them off."
"Jack, you're sturdy and alert. You'll provide cover fire and guard the rear."

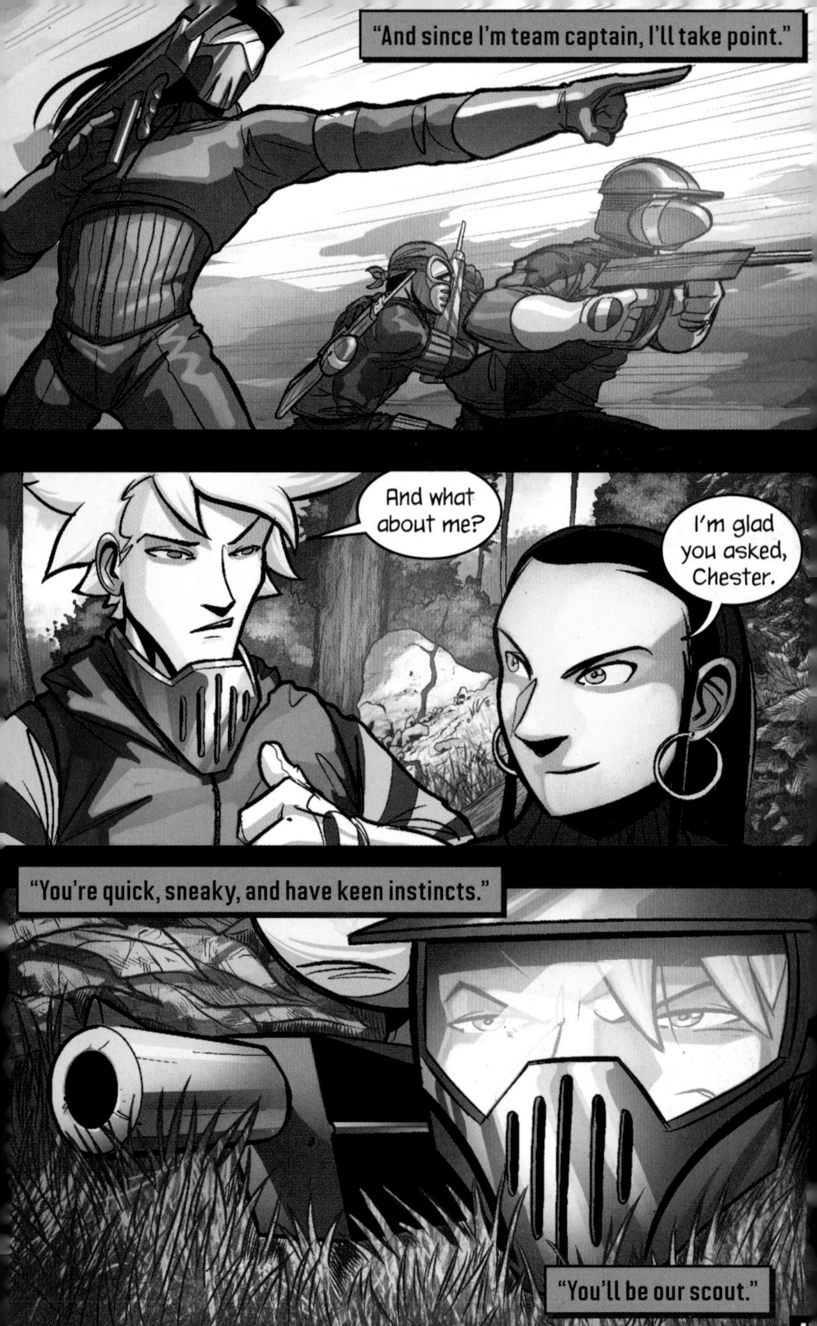
"And since I'm team captain, I'll take point."
And what about me?
I'm glad you asked, Chester.
"You're quick, sneaky, and have keen instincts."
"You'll be our scout."

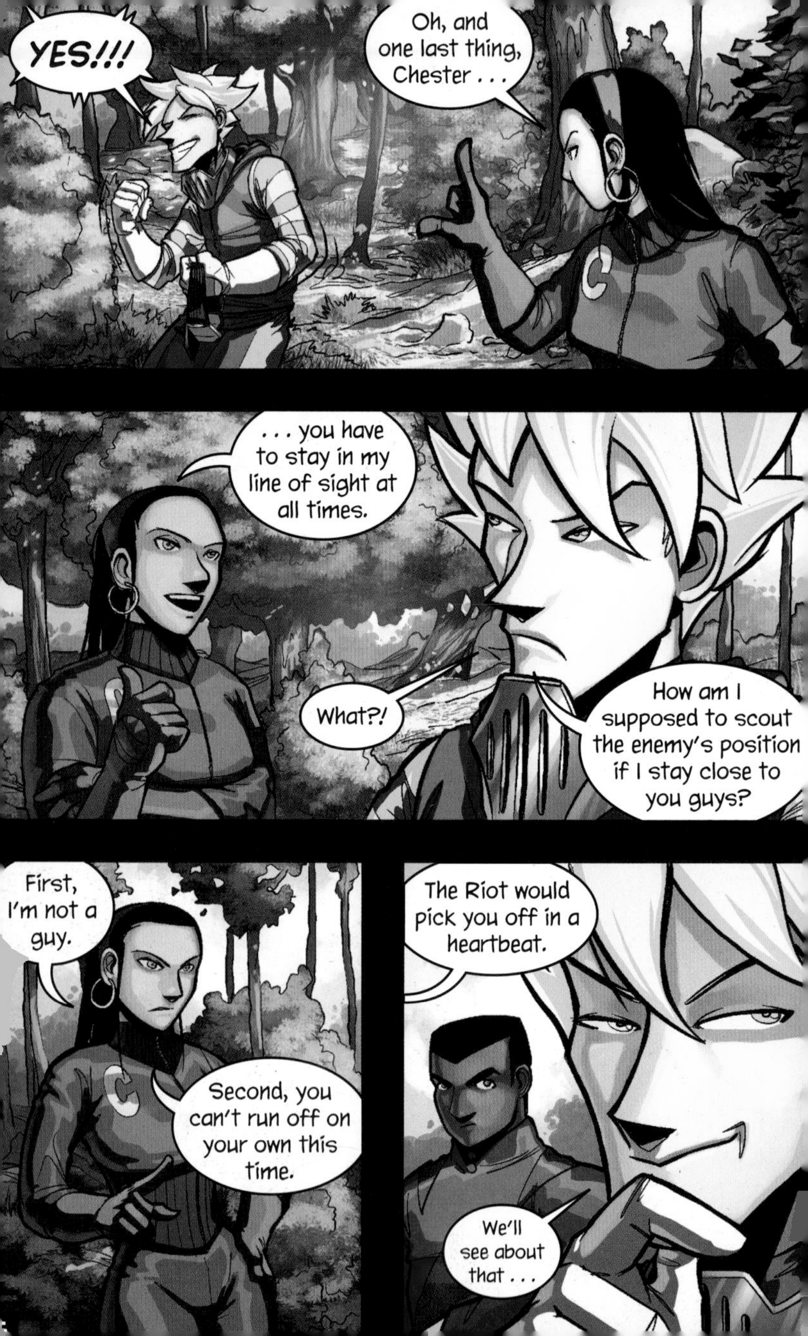
YES!!!
Oh, and one last thing, Chester . . .
. . . you have to stay in my line of sight at all times.
What?!
How am I supposed to scout the enemy's position if I stay close to you guys?
First, I'm not a guy.
Second, you can't run off on your own this time.
The Riot would pick you off in a heartbeat.
We'll see about that . . .

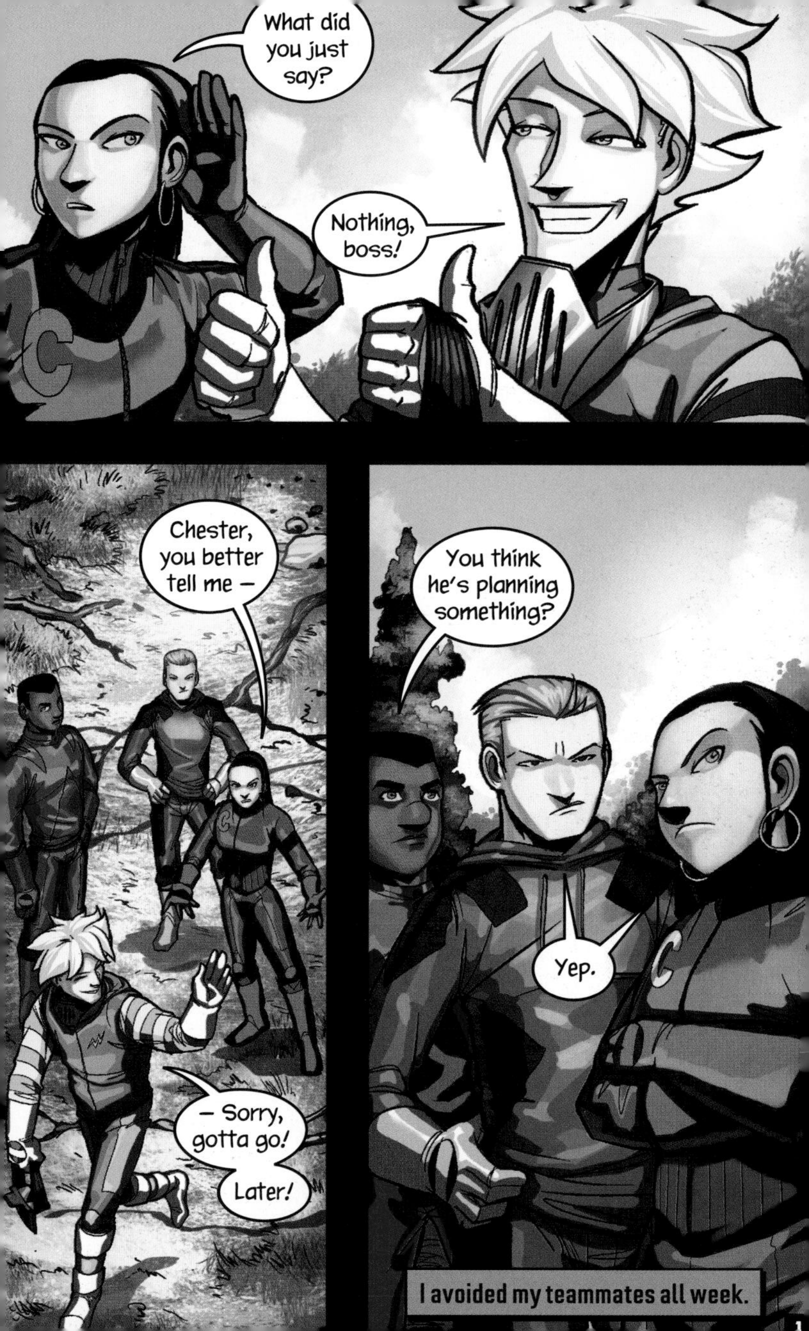
What did you just say?
Nothing, boss!
Chester, you better tell me —
— Sorry, gotta go!
Later!
You think he's planning something?
Yep.
I avoided my teammates all week.

The next time I saw them, we were facing the Riot in the state paintball championship.

Okay, Wolves. Here's the plan of attack . . .

First, we'll . . .

Jack will cover . . .

Then Peter . . .

Blee blah bloo-dee-dah.

Blee blah bo-dee-dah. a-dee-dah. Blah.

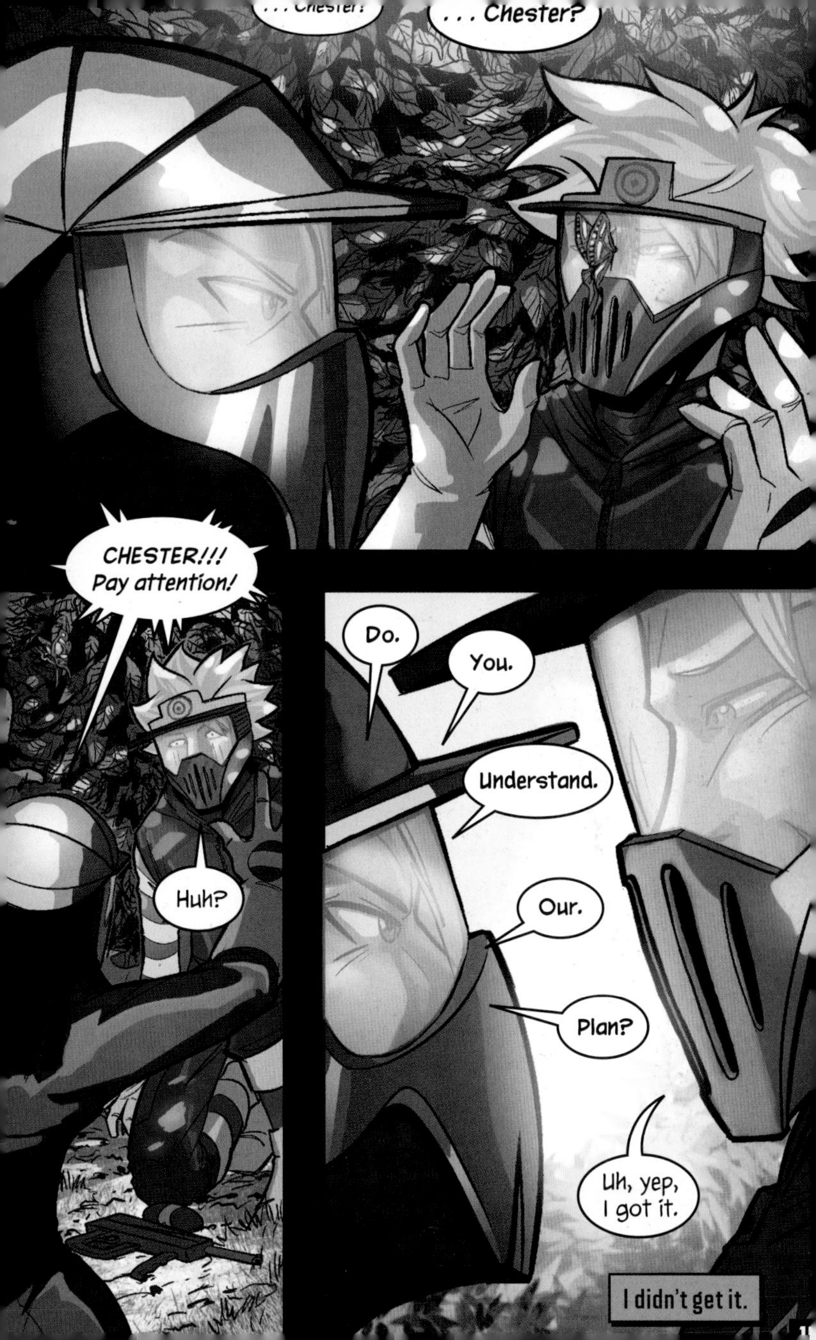
. . . Chester?
CHESTER!!! Pay attention!
Huh?
Do.
You.
Understand.
Our.
Plan?
Uh, yep, I got it.
I didn't get it.

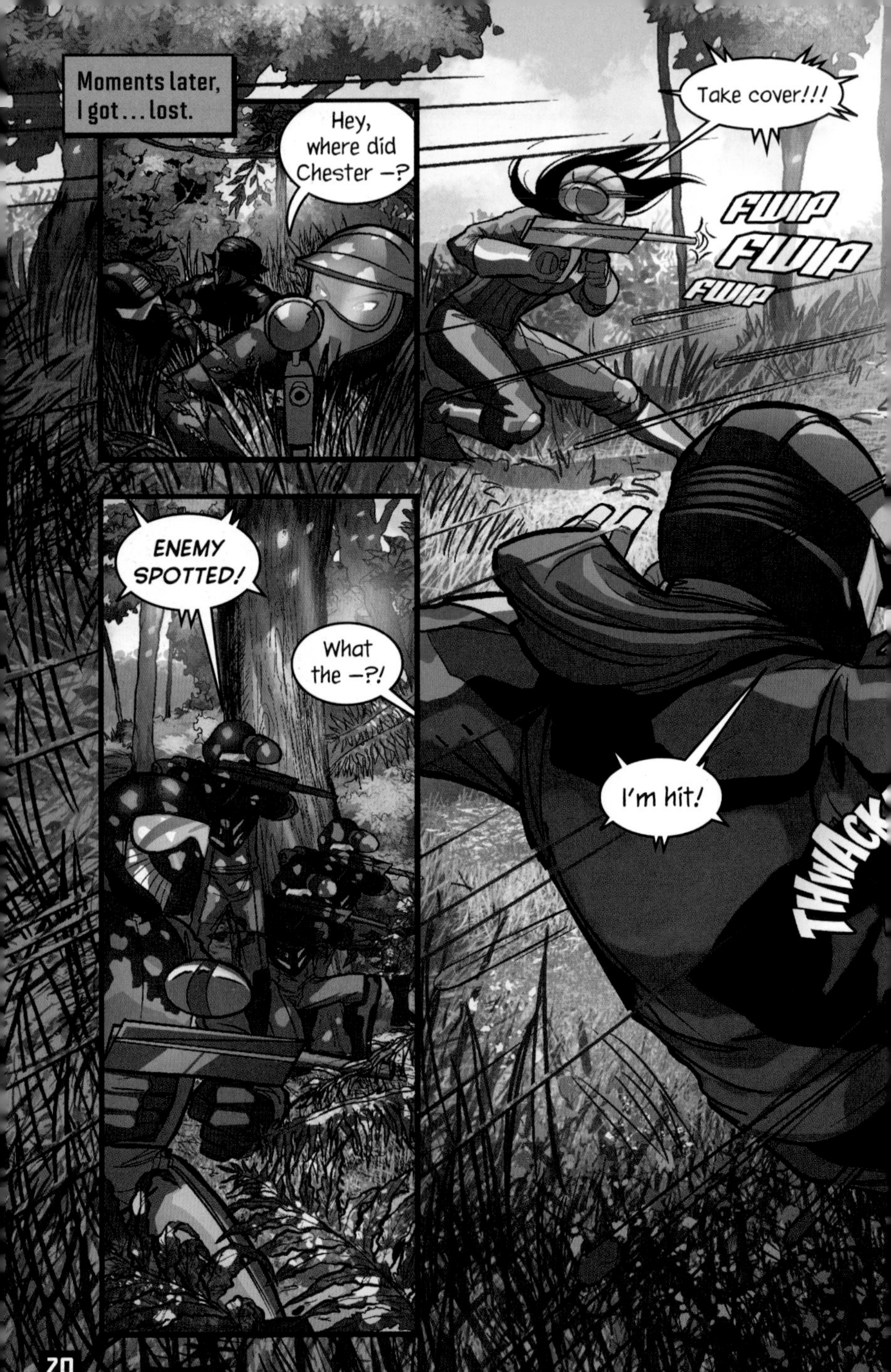

Moments later, I got . . . lost.
Hey, where did Chester –?
Take cover!!!
FWIP
FWIP
FWIP
ENEMY SPOTTED!
What the –?!
I'm hit!
THWACK

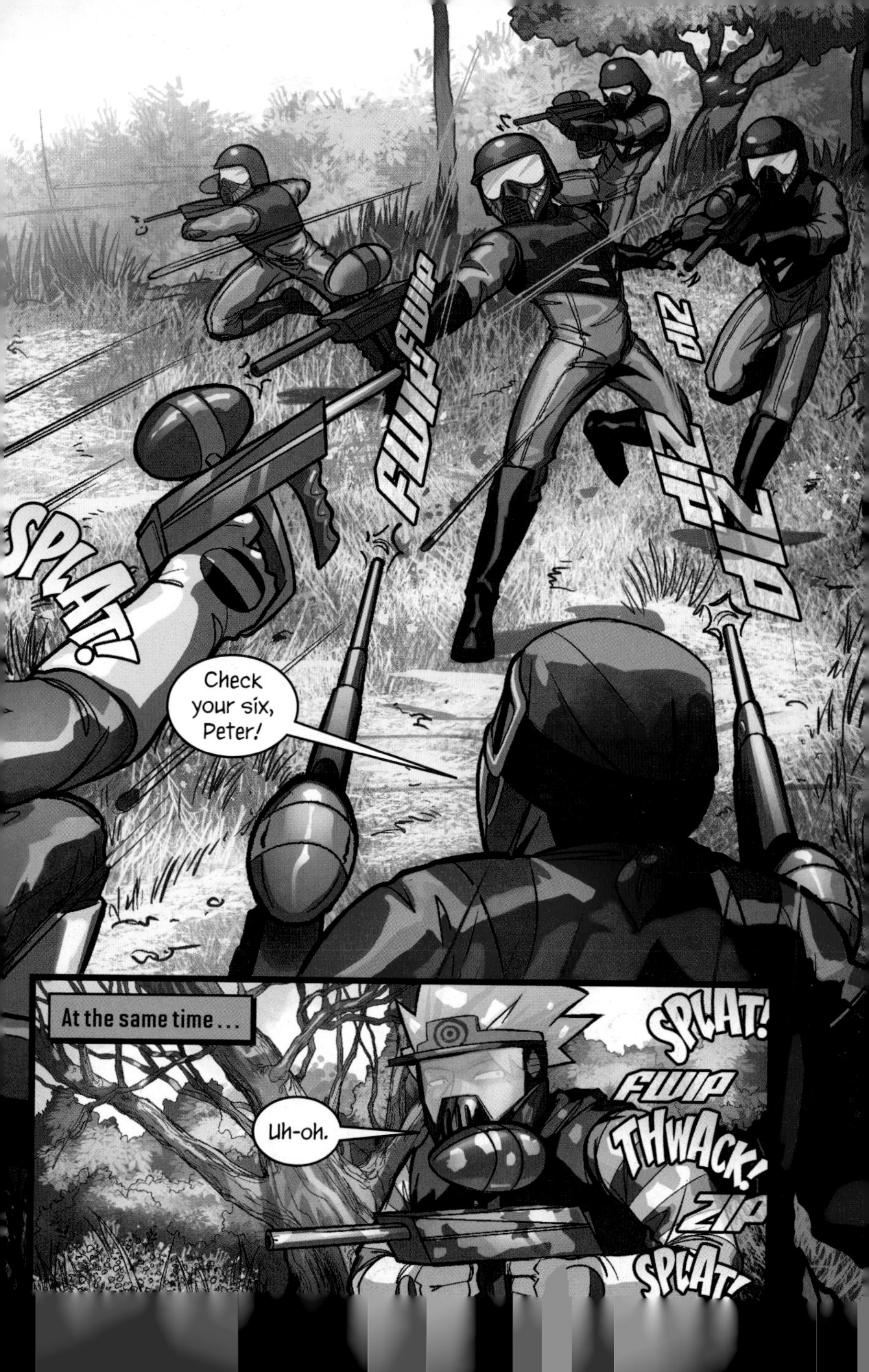
FWIP FWIP
ZIP
ZIP ZIP
SPLAT!
Check your six, Peter!
At the same time . . .
SPLAT!
Uh-oh.
FWIP
THWACK!
ZIP
SPLAT!

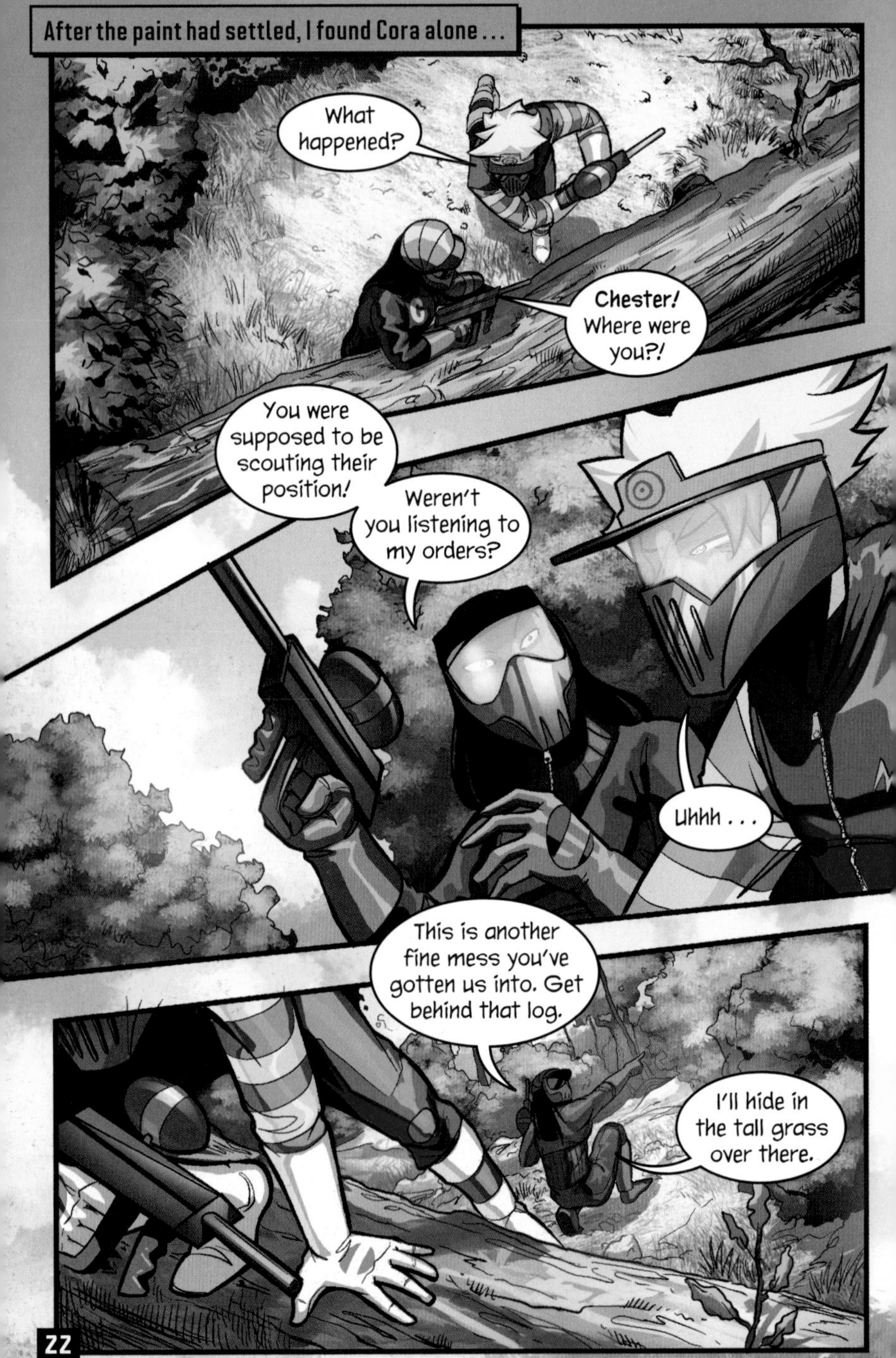
After the paint had settled, I found Cora alone . . .
What happened?
Chester! Where were you?!
You were supposed to be scouting their position!
Weren't you listening to my orders?
Uhhh . . .
This is another fine mess you've gotten us into. Get behind that log.
I'll hide in the tall grass over there.

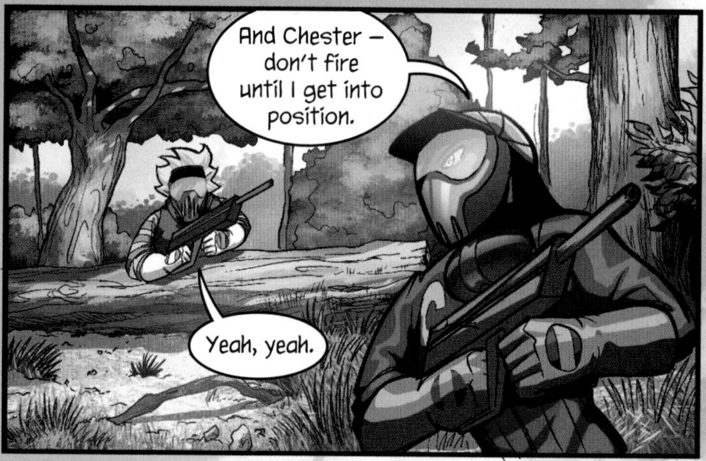

And Chester — don't fire until I get into position.
Yeah, yeah.

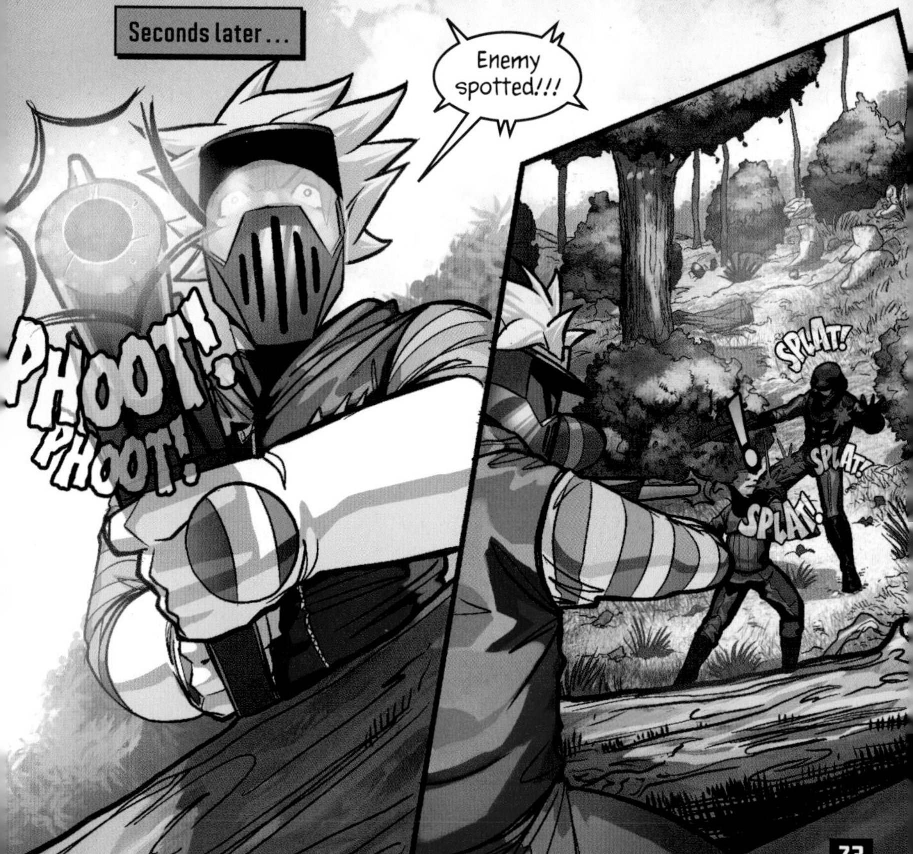

Seconds later . . .
Enemy spotted!!!
PHOOT!
PHOOT!
SPLAT!
SPLAT!
SPLAT!
!

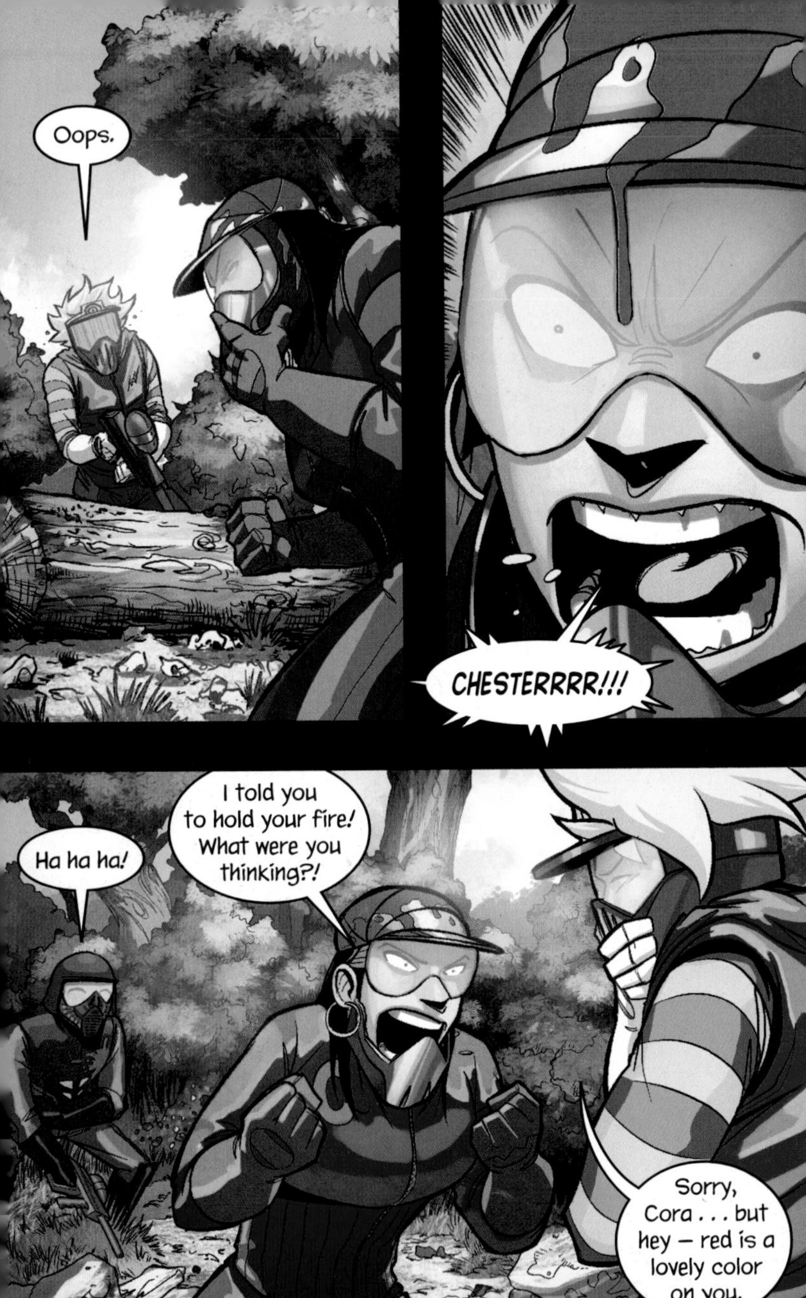
Oops.
CHESTERRRR!!!
Ha ha ha!
I told you to hold your fire! What were you thinking?!
Sorry, Cora . . . but hey — red is a lovely color on you.

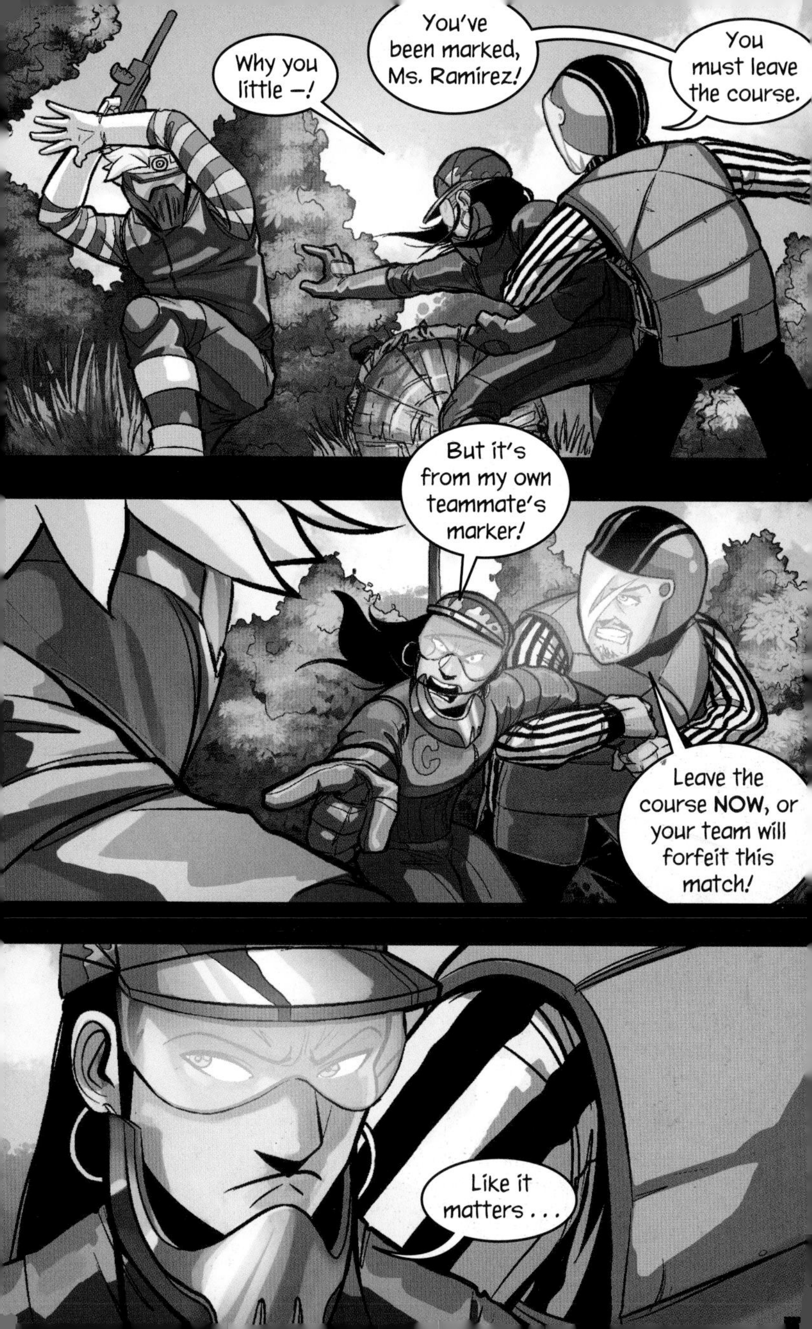
Why you little —!
You've been marked, Ms. Ramirez!
You must leave the course.
But it's from my own teammate's marker!
Leave the course NOW, or your team will forfeit this match!
Like it matters . . .

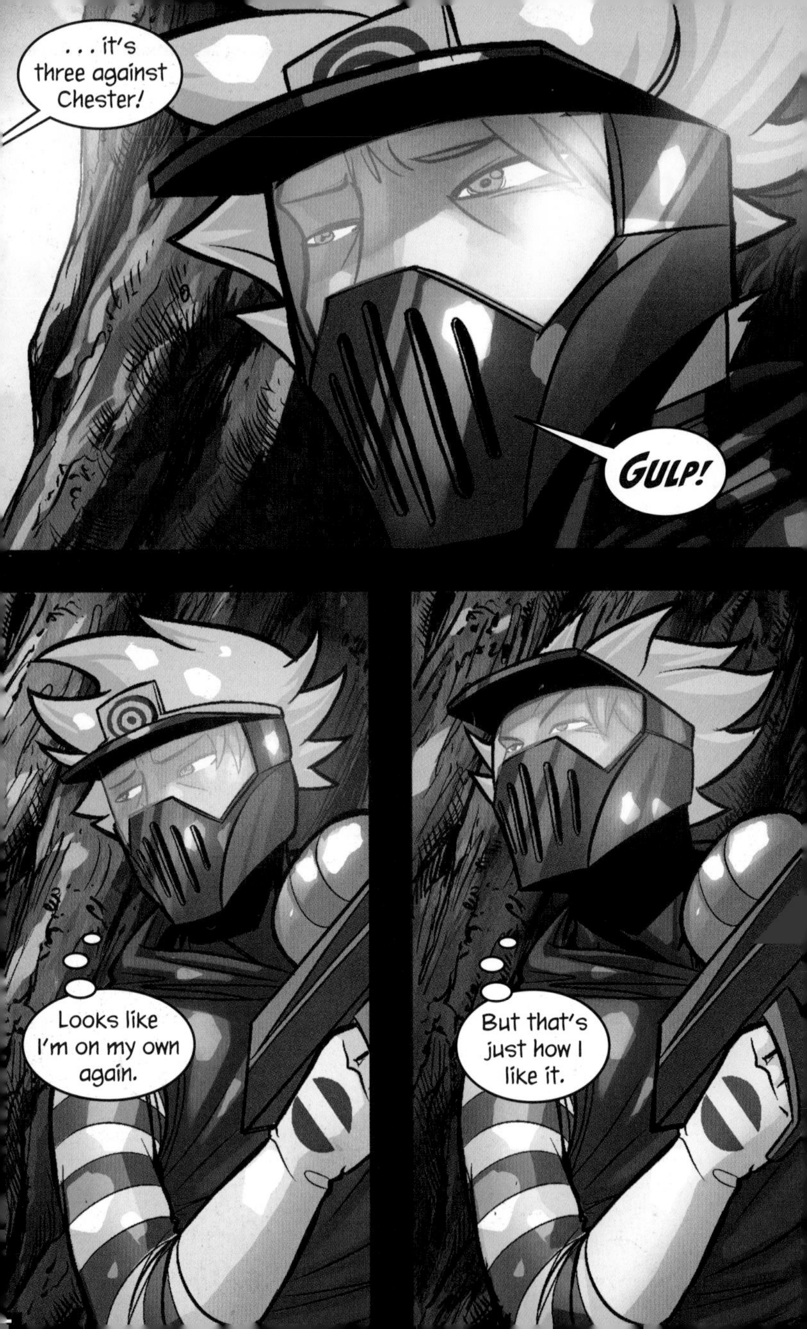
. . . it's three against Chester!
GULP!
Looks like I'm on my own again.
But that's just how I like it.

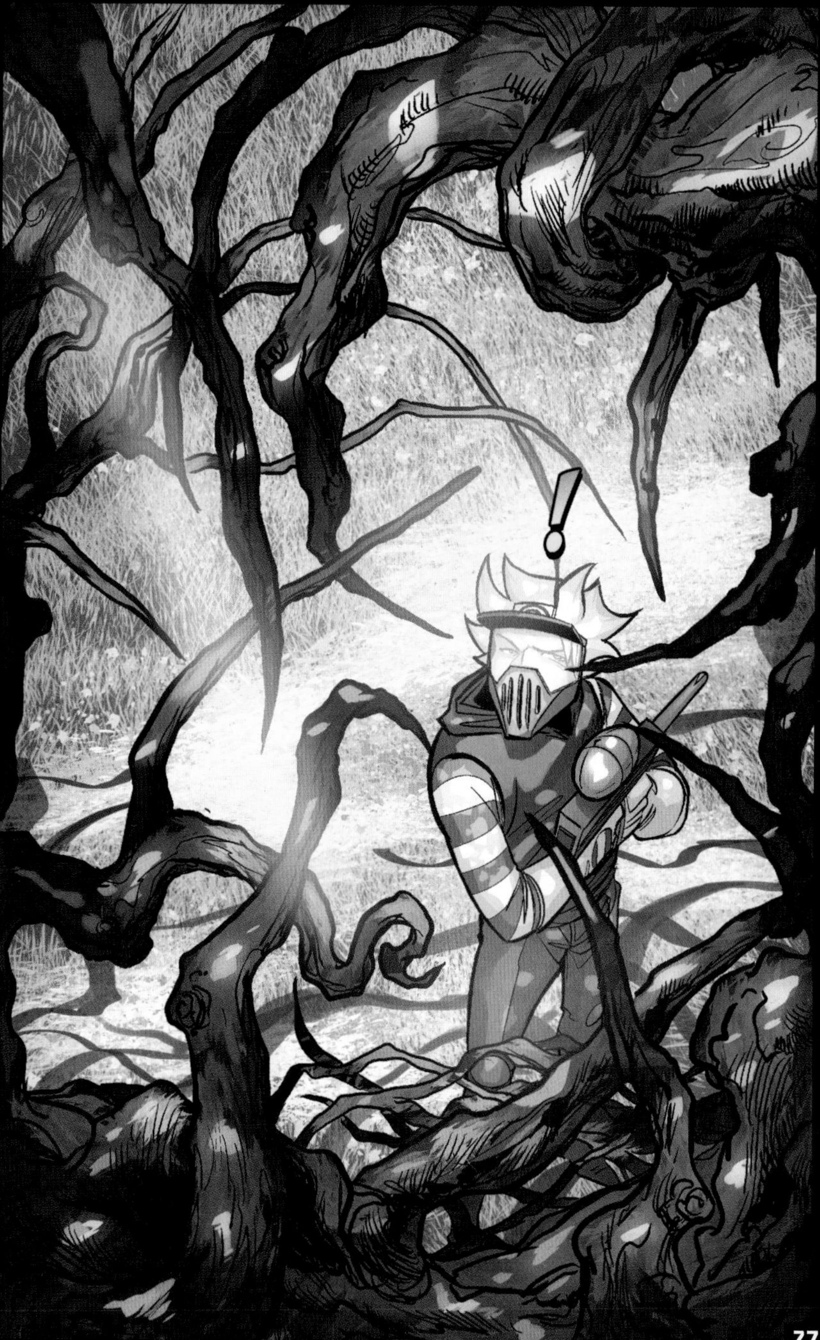
!

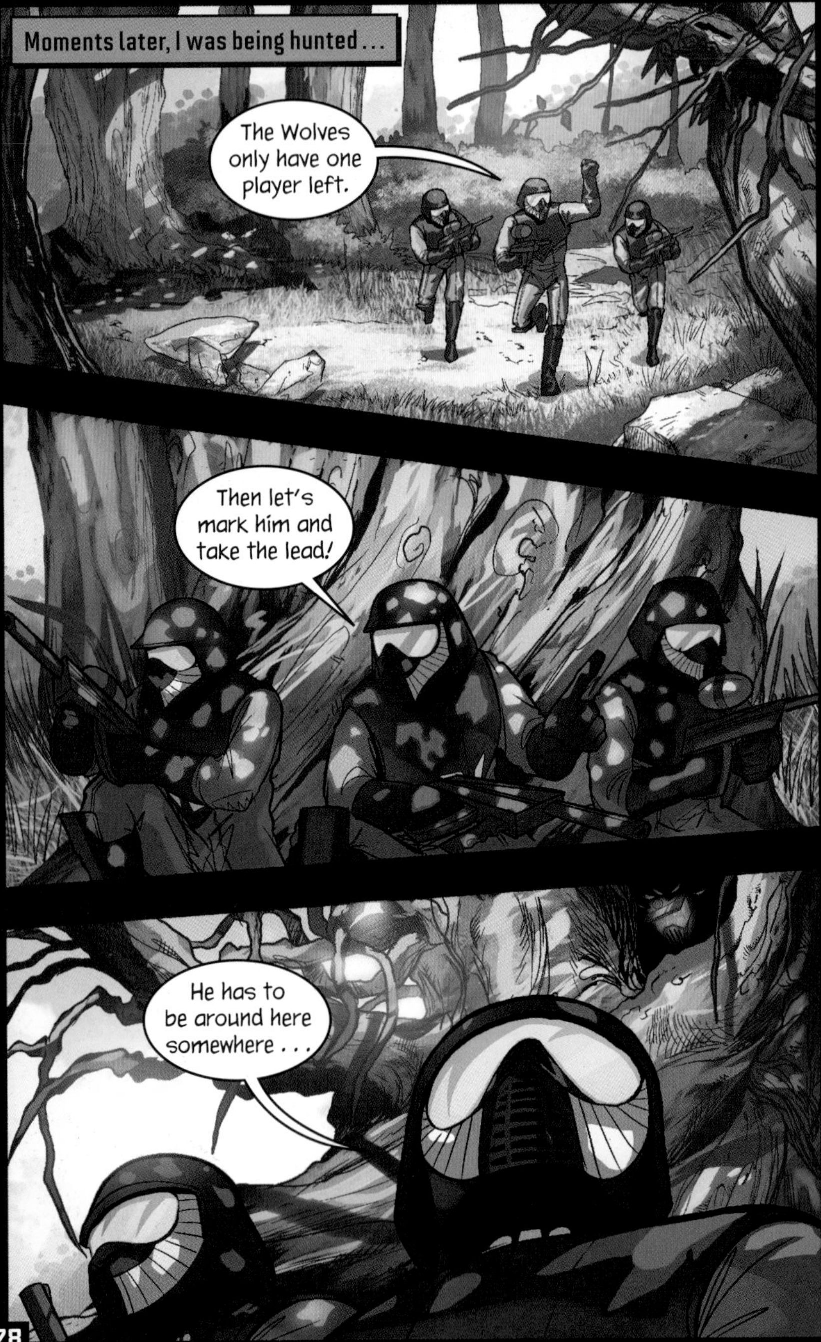
Moments later, I was being hunted . . .
The Wolves only have one player left.
Then let's mark him and take the lead!
He has to be around here somewhere . . .

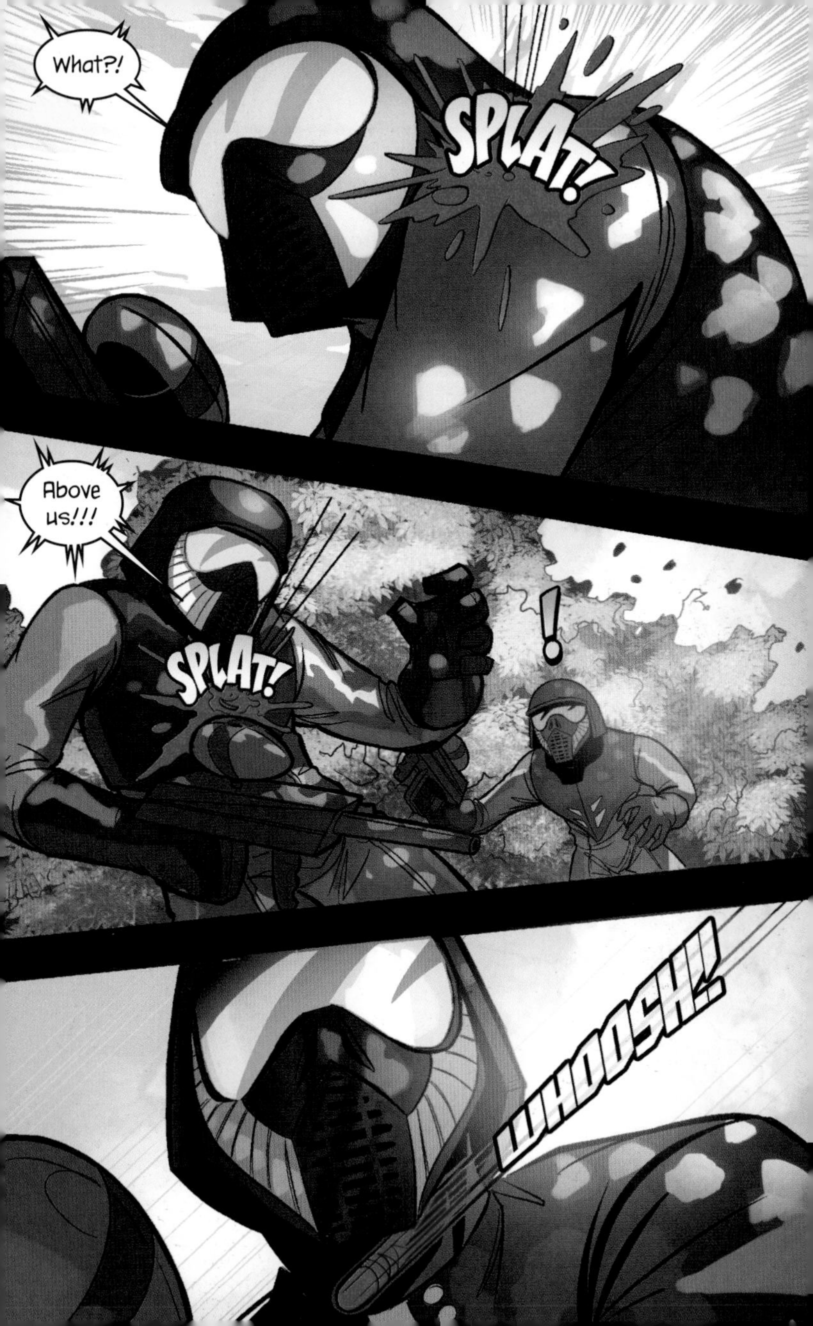
What?!
SPLAT!
Above us!!!
SPLAT!
!
WHOOSH!!

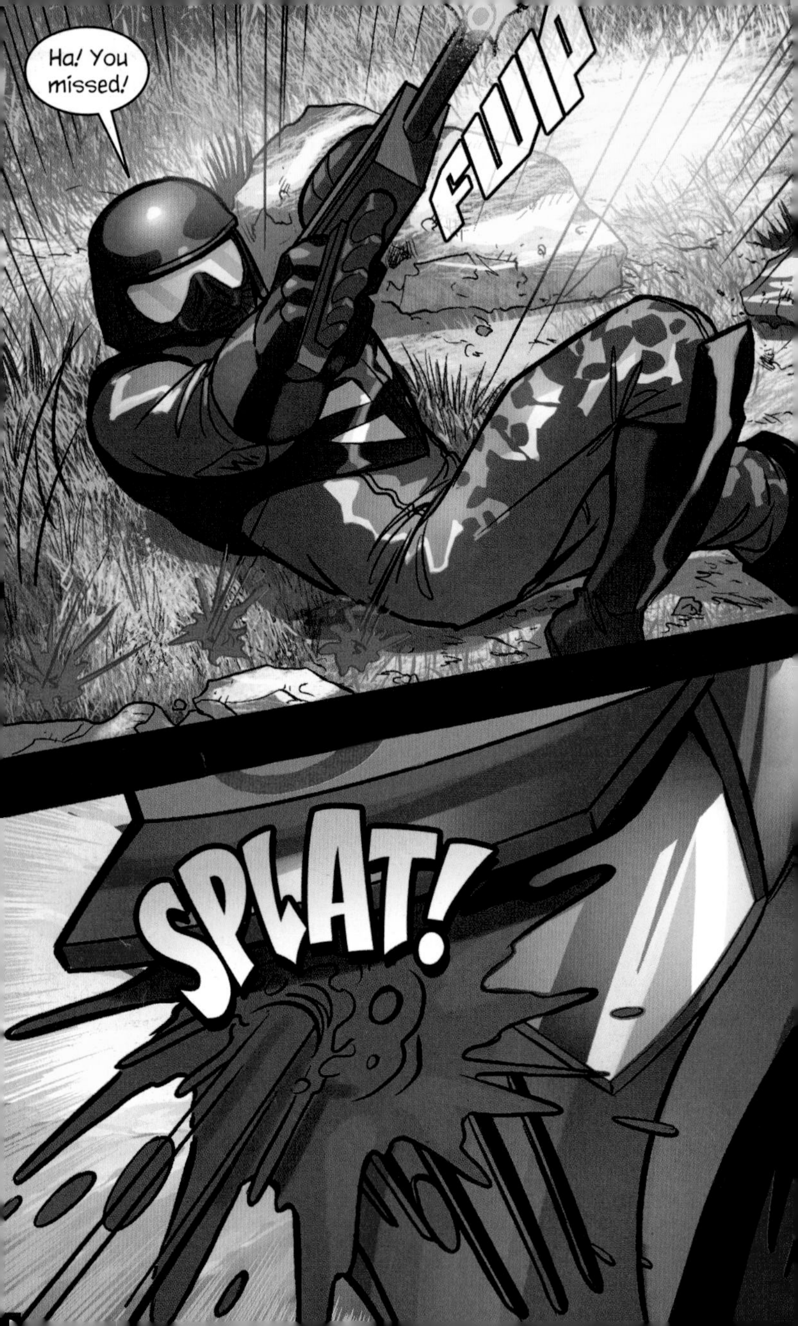
Ha! You missed!
FUUP
SPLAT!

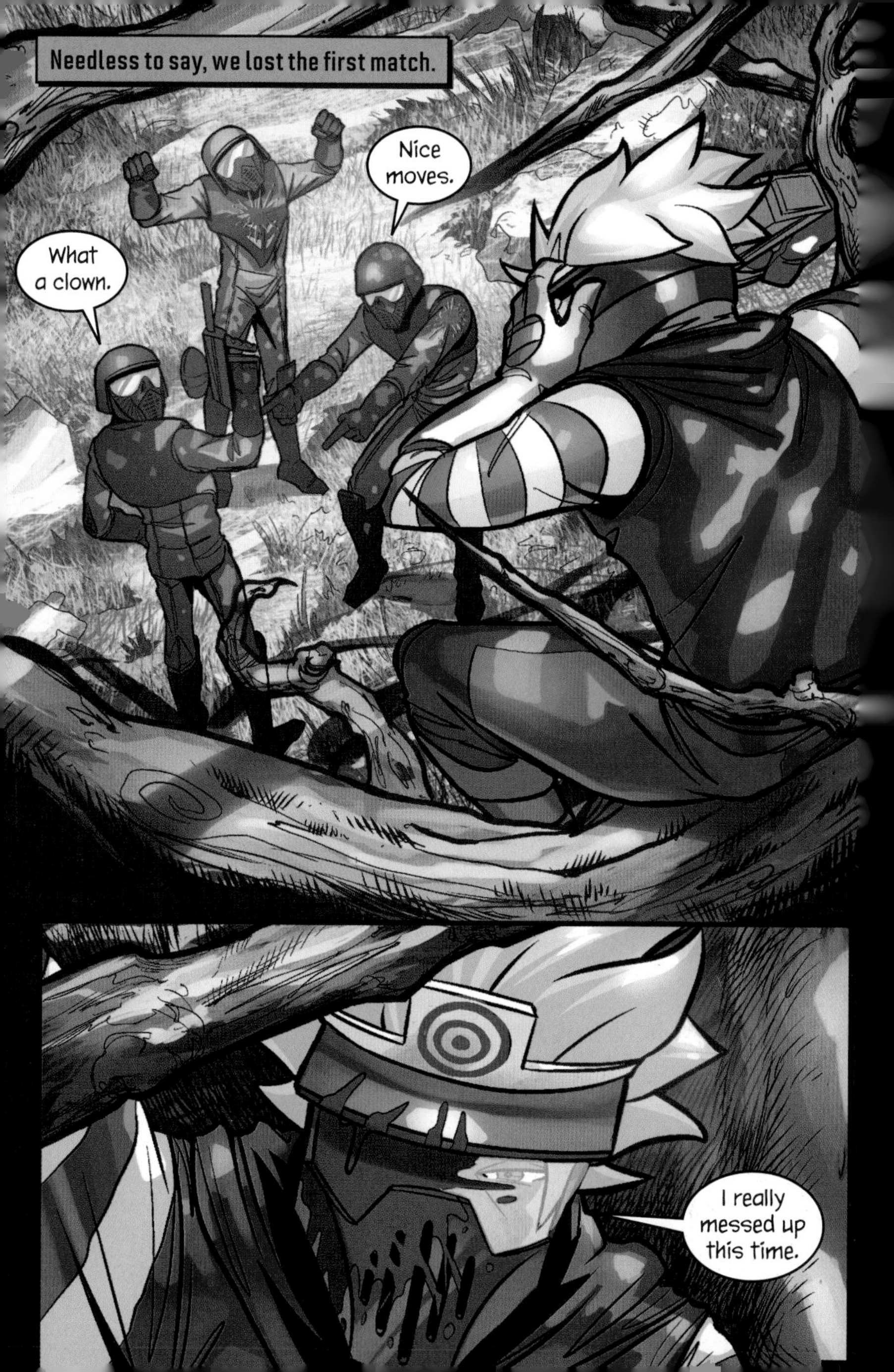
Needless to say, we lost the first match.
Nice moves.
What a clown.
I really messed up this time.

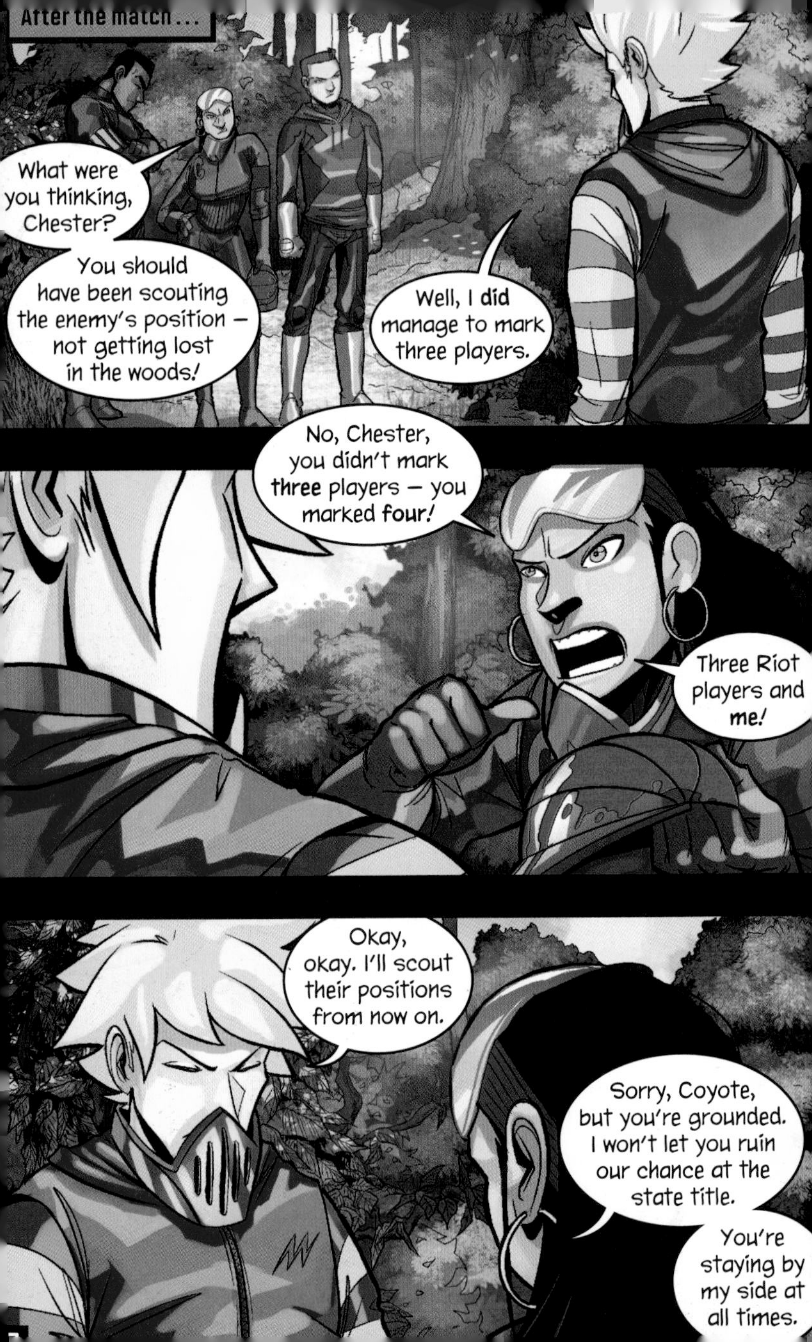
After the match . . .
What were you thinking, Chester?
You should have been scouting the enemy's position — not getting lost in the woods!
Well, I did manage to mark three players.
No, Chester, you didn't mark three players — you marked four!
Three Riot players and me!
Okay, okay. I'll scout their positions from now on.
Sorry, Coyote, but you're grounded. I won't let you ruin our chance at the state title.
You're staying by my side at all times.

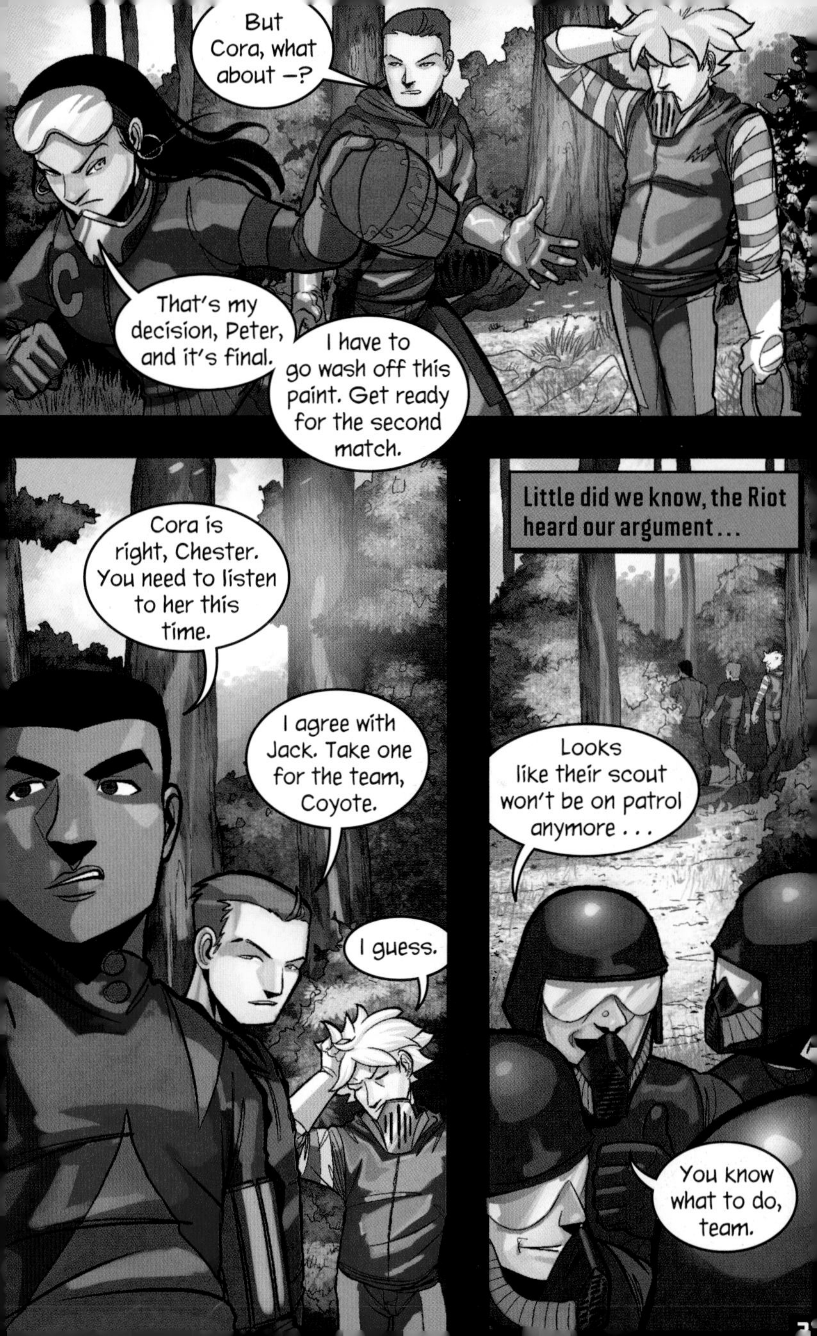
But Cora, what about —?
That's my decision, Peter, and it's final.
I have to go wash off this paint. Get ready for the second match.
Cora is right, Chester. You need to listen to her this time.
I agree with Jack. Take one for the team, Coyote.
I guess.
Little did we know, the Riot heard our argument . . .
Looks like their scout won't be on patrol anymore . . .
You know what to do, team.

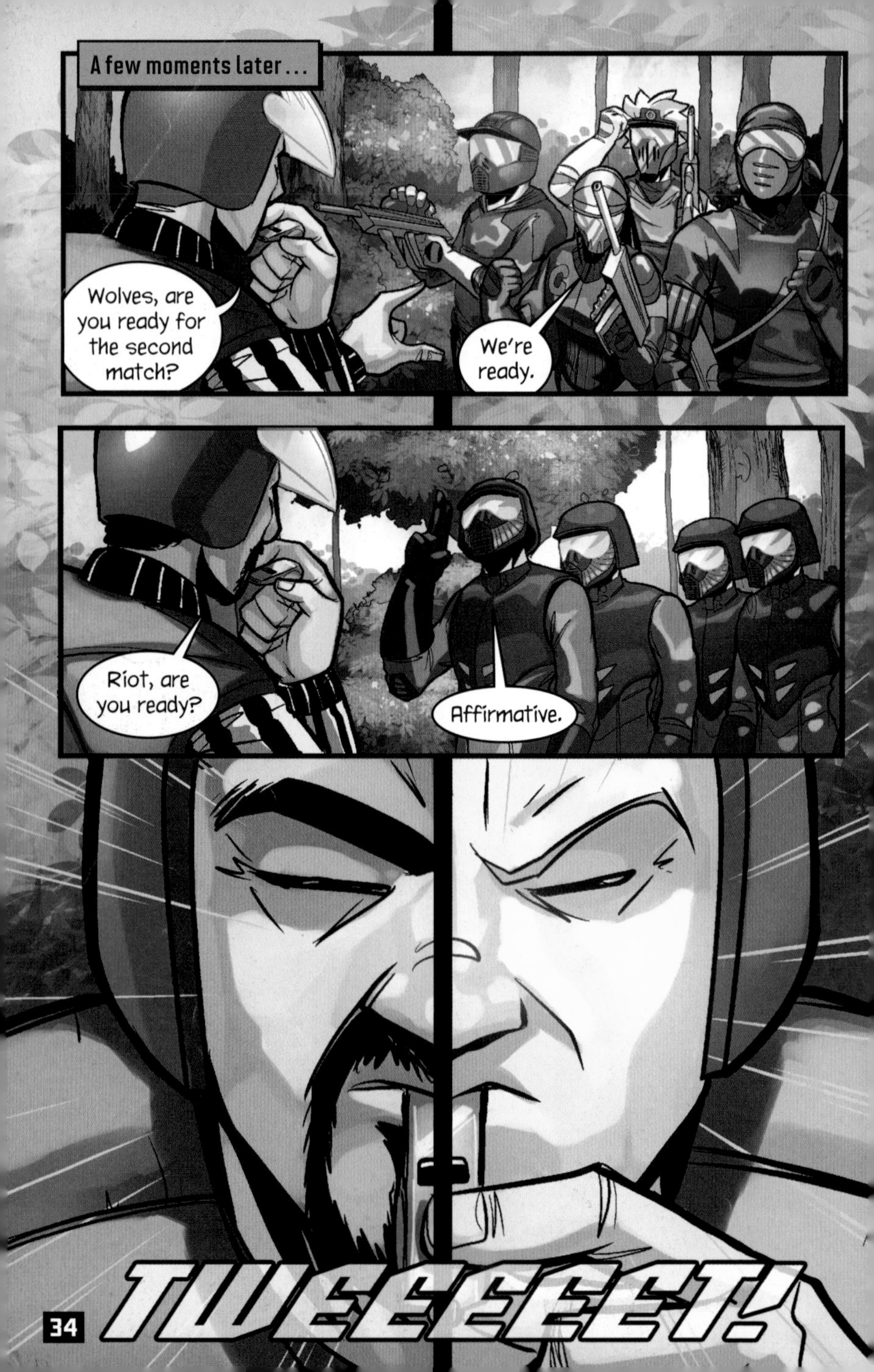
A few moments later . . .
Wolves, are you ready for the second match?
We're ready.
Riot, are you ready?
Affirmative.
TWEEEEET!

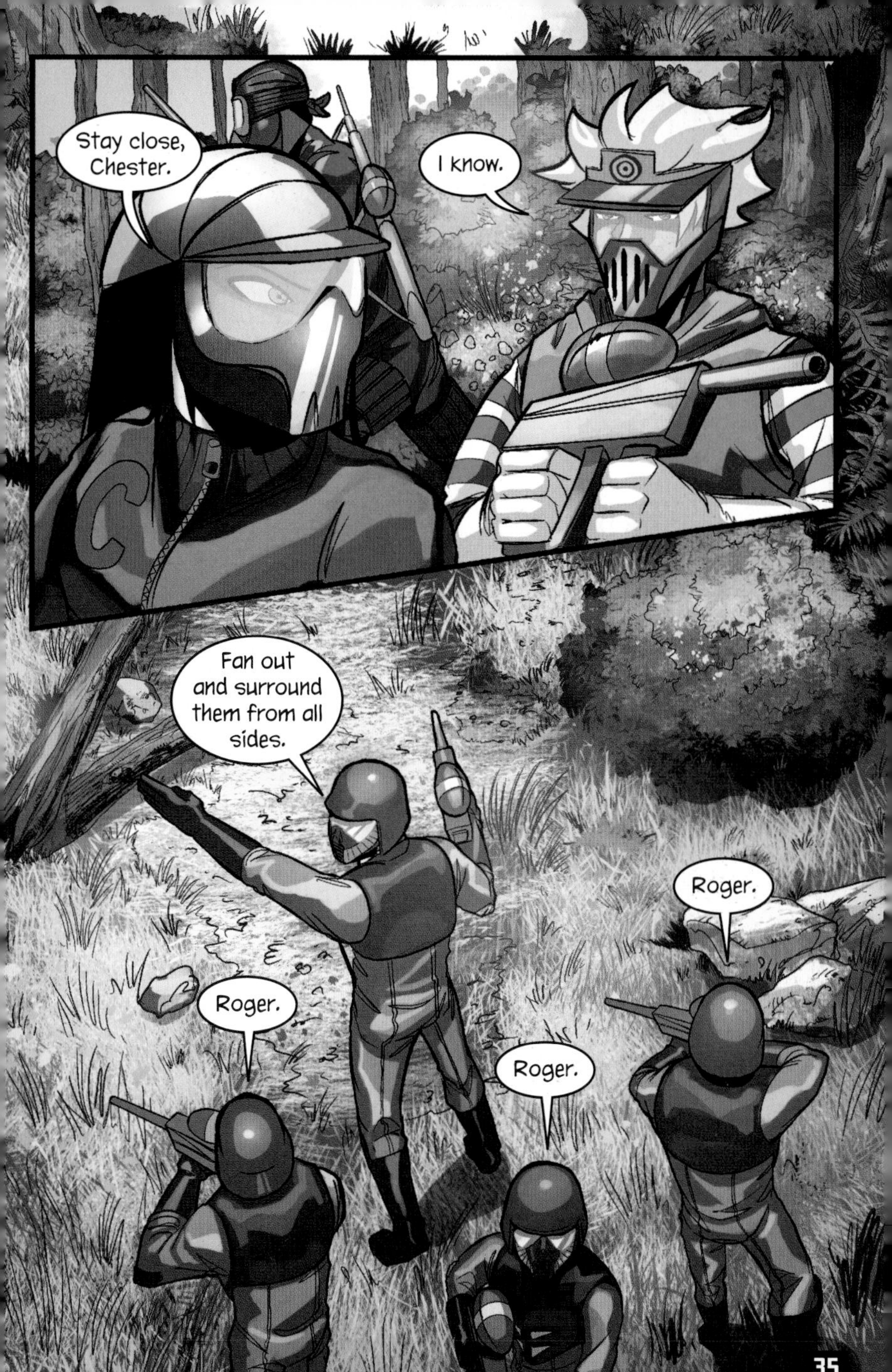
Stay close, Chester.
I know.
Fan out and surround them from all sides.
Roger.
Roger.
Roger.

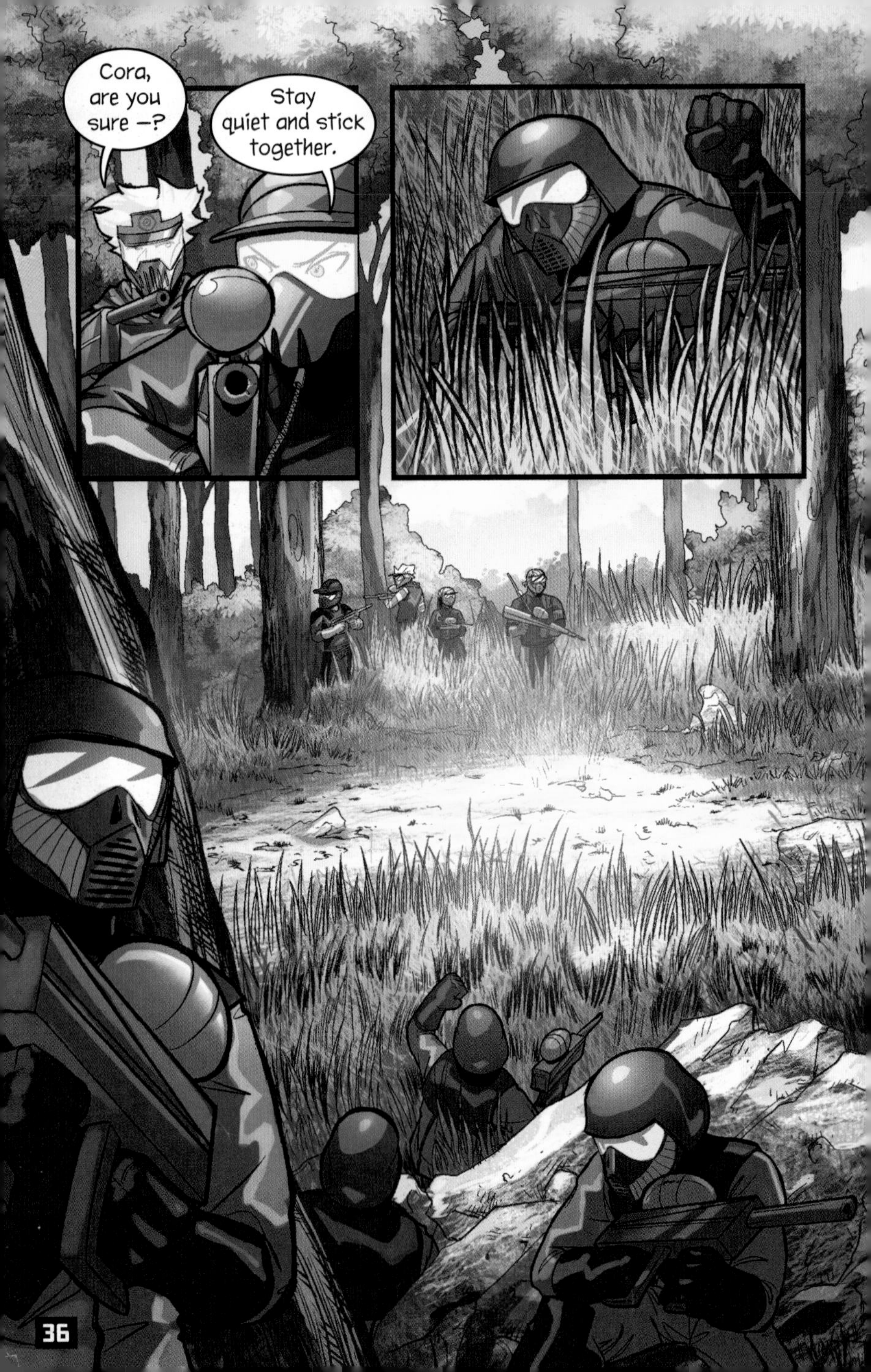
Cora, are you sure —?
Stay quiet and stick together.

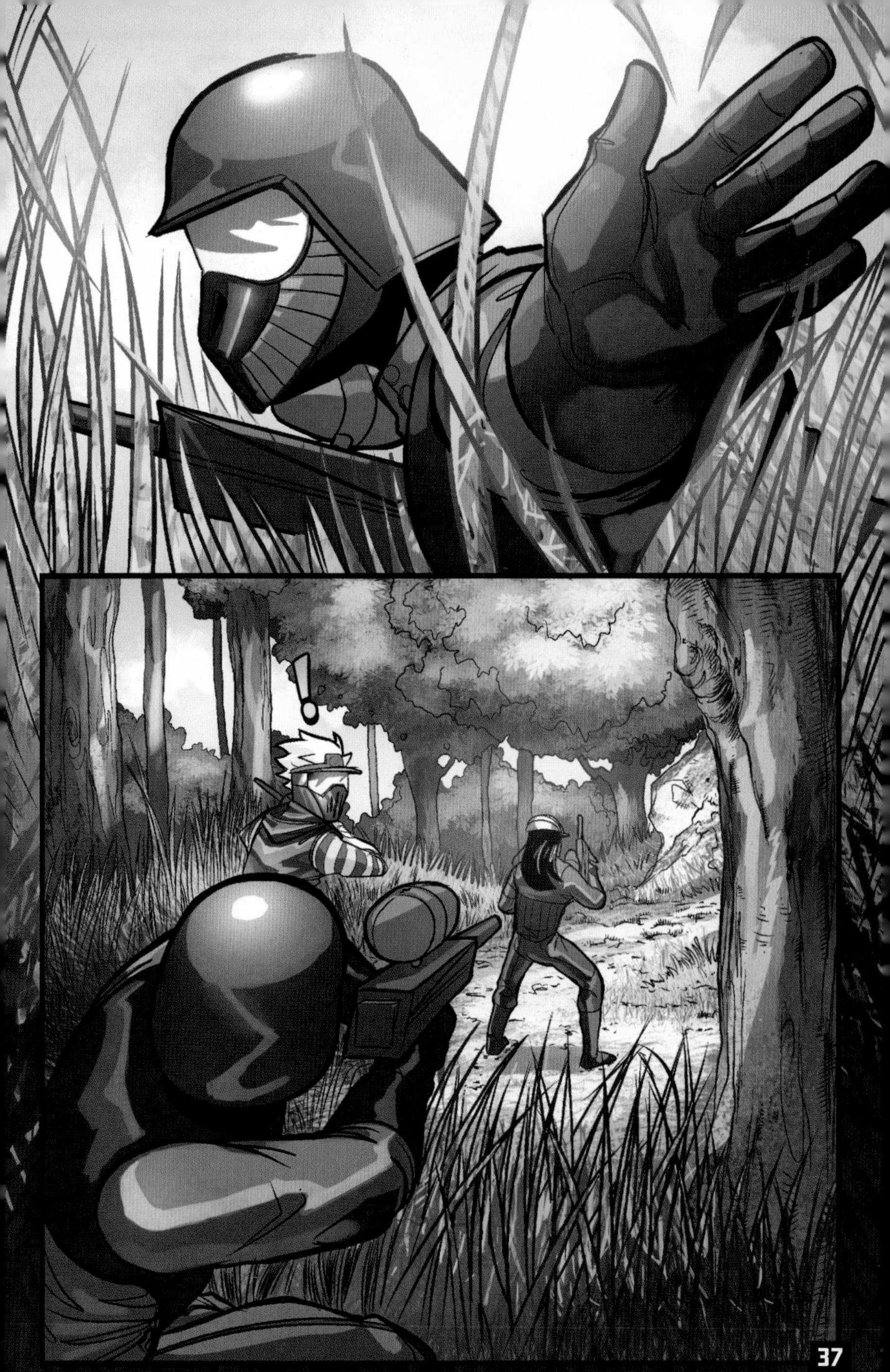
!

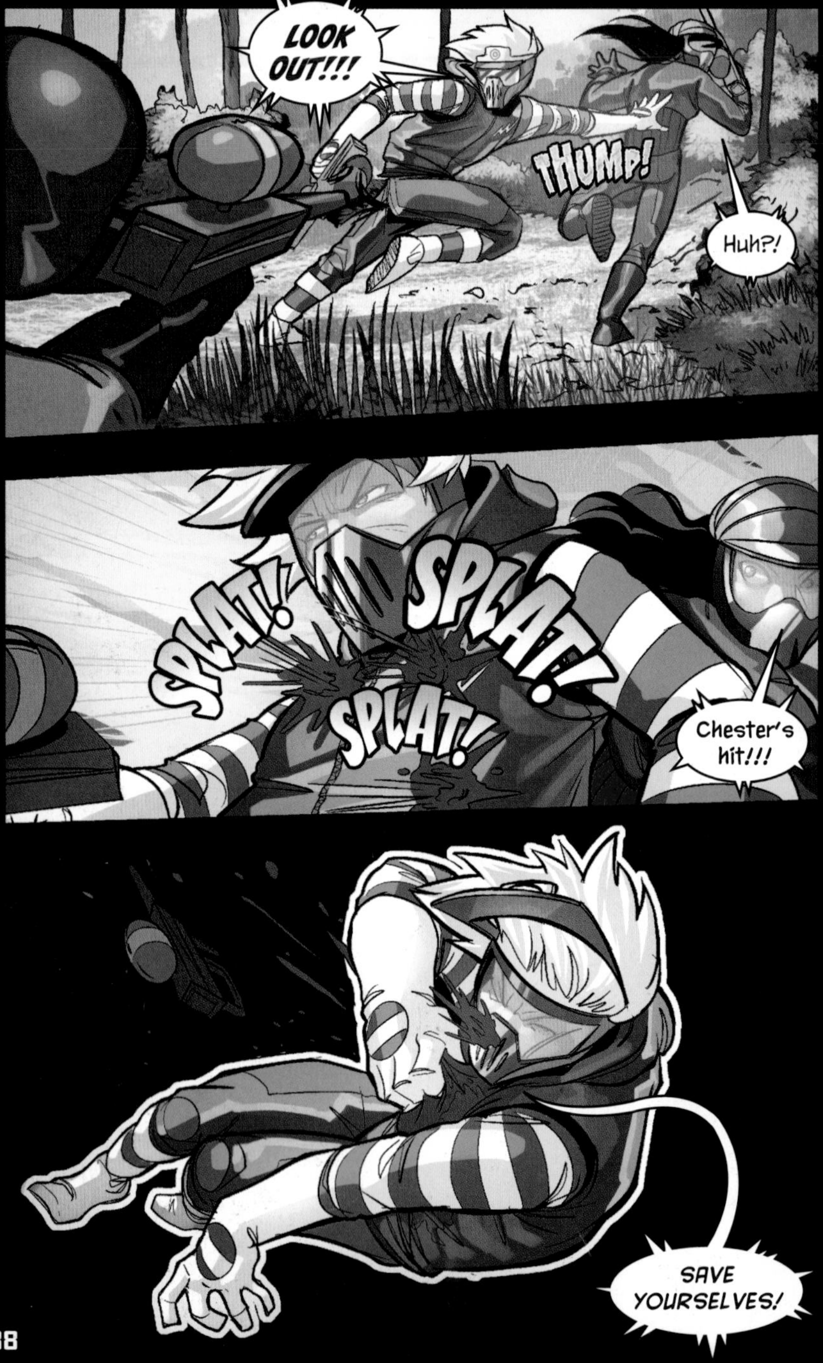
LOOK OUT!!!
THUMP!
Huh?!
SPLAT!
SPLAT!
SPLAT!
Chester's hit!!!
SAVE YOURSELVES!

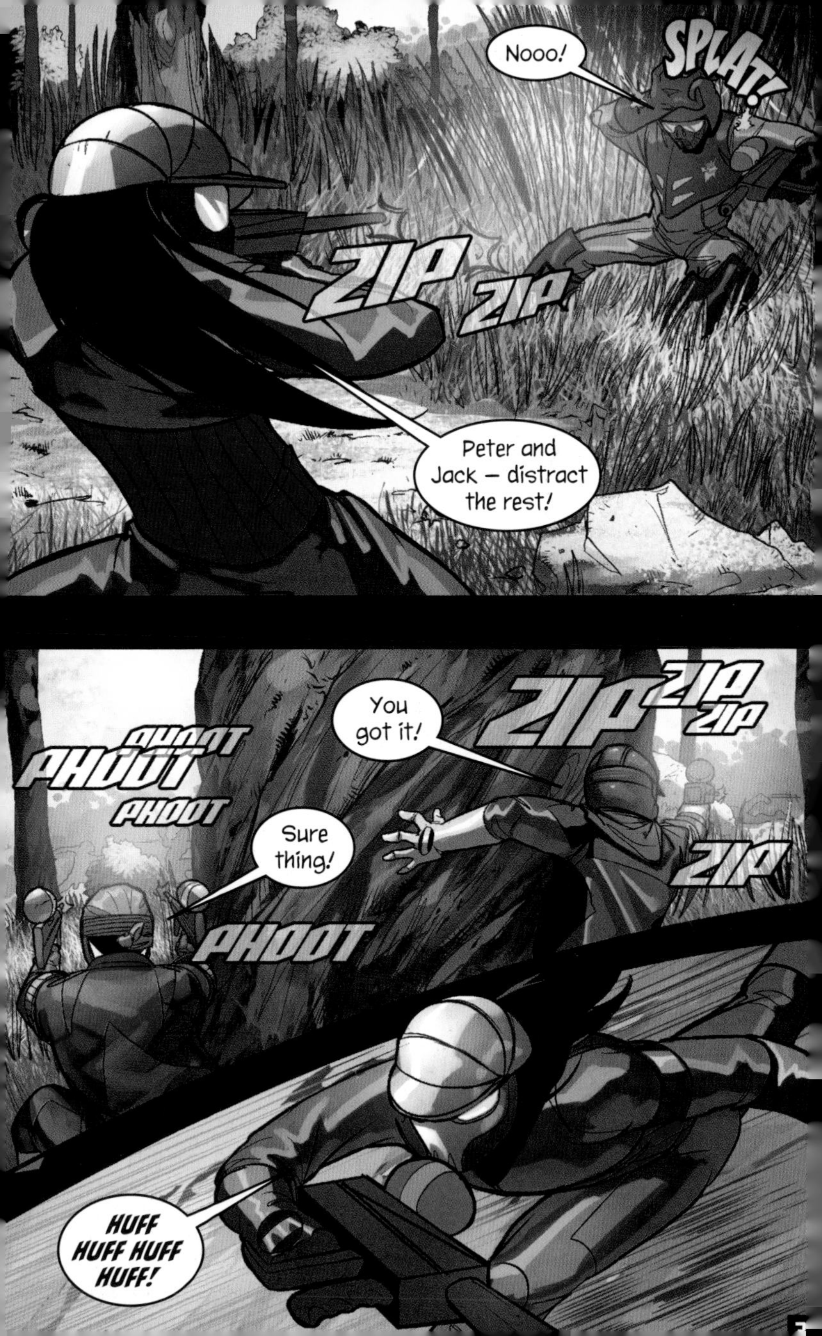
Nooo!
SPLAT!
ZIP ZIP
Peter and Jack – distract the rest!
ZIP ZIP ZIP
You got it!
PHOOT PHOOT PHOOT
Sure thing!
ZIP
PHOOT
HUFF HUFF HUFF HUFF!

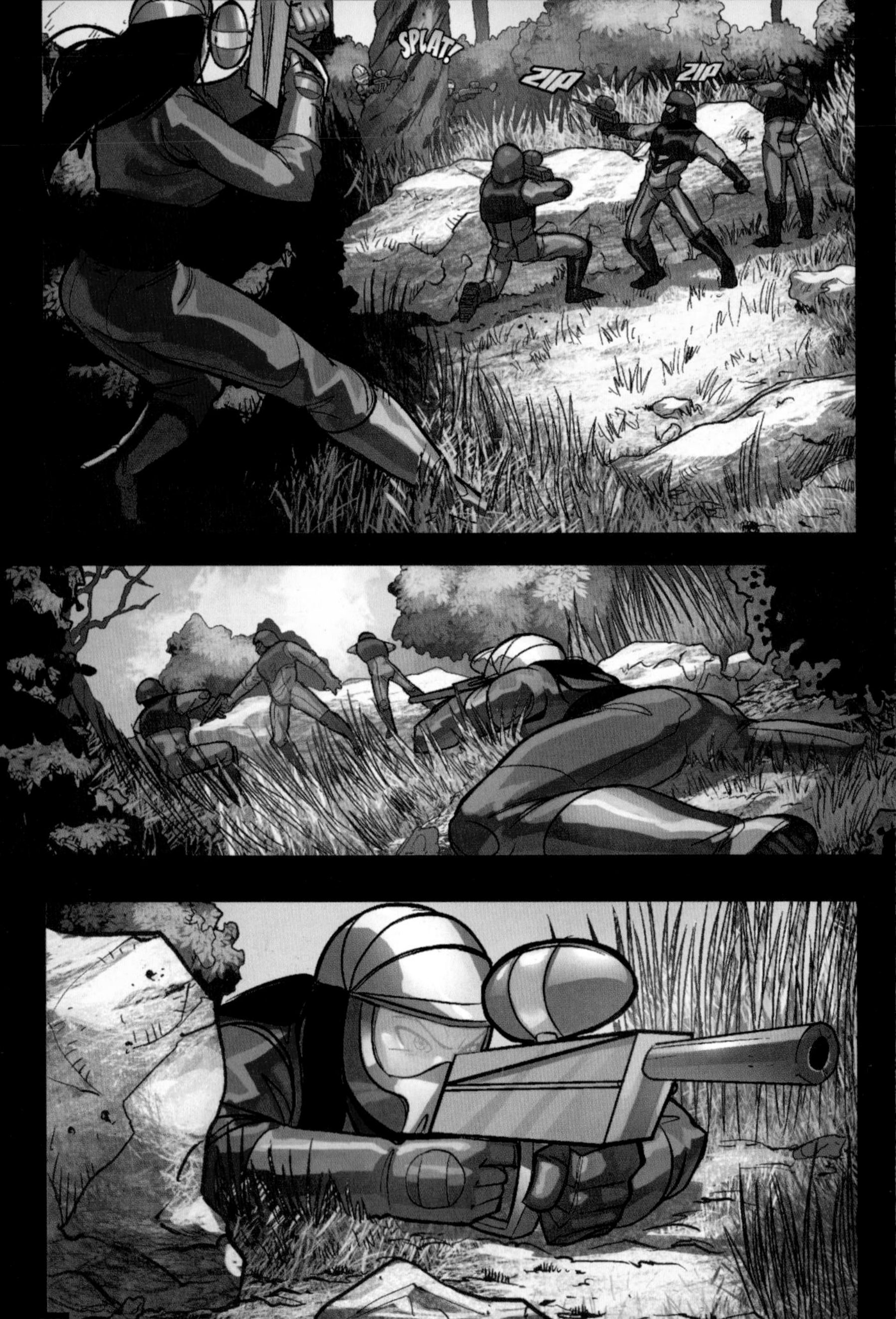
SPLAT!
ZIP
ZIP

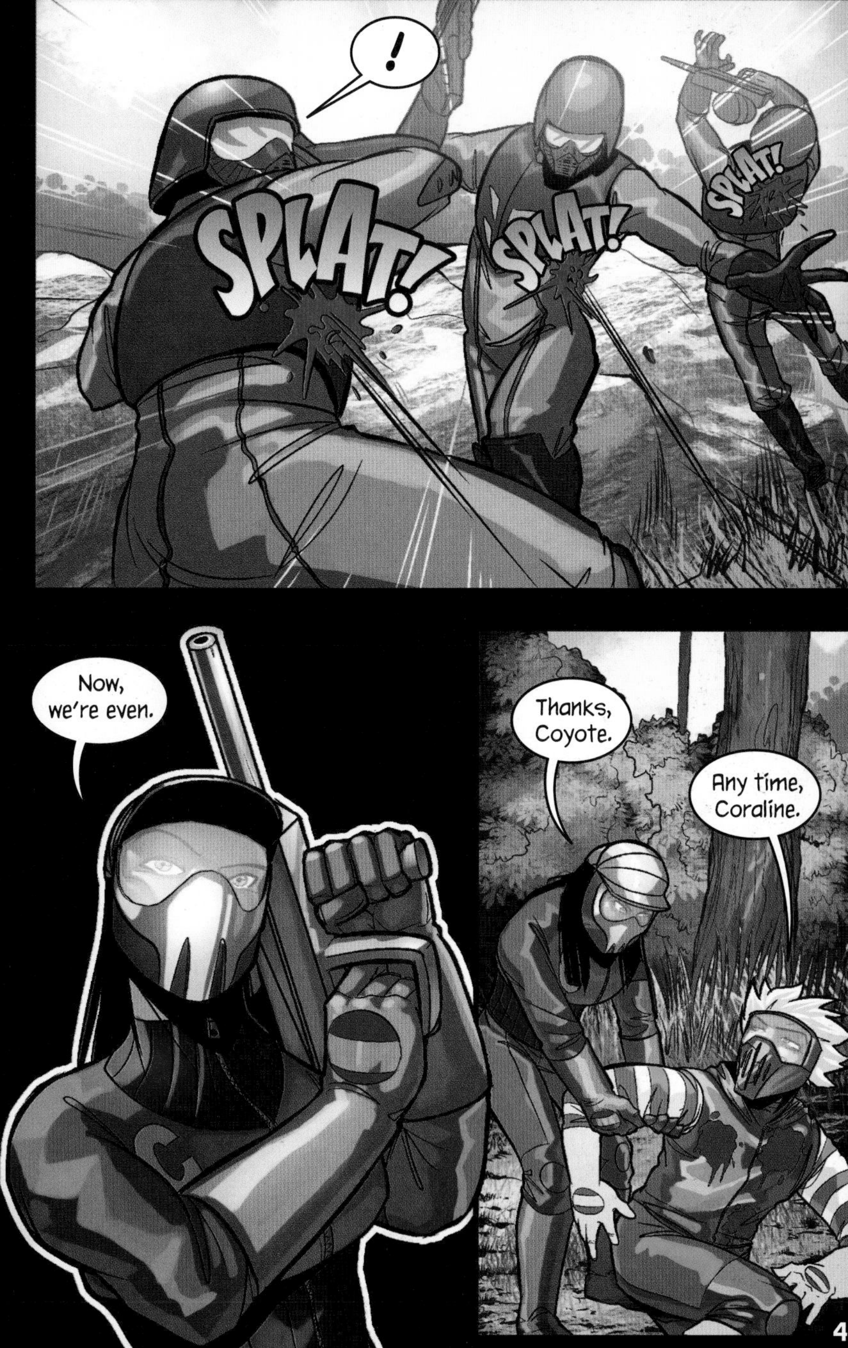
!
SPLAT!
SPLAT!
SPLAT!
Now, we're even.
Thanks, Coyote.
Any time, Coraline.

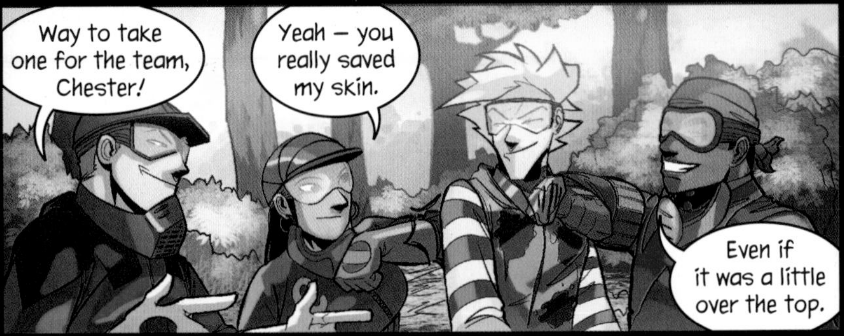
Way to take one for the team, Chester!
Yeah — you really saved my skin.
Even if it was a little over the top.

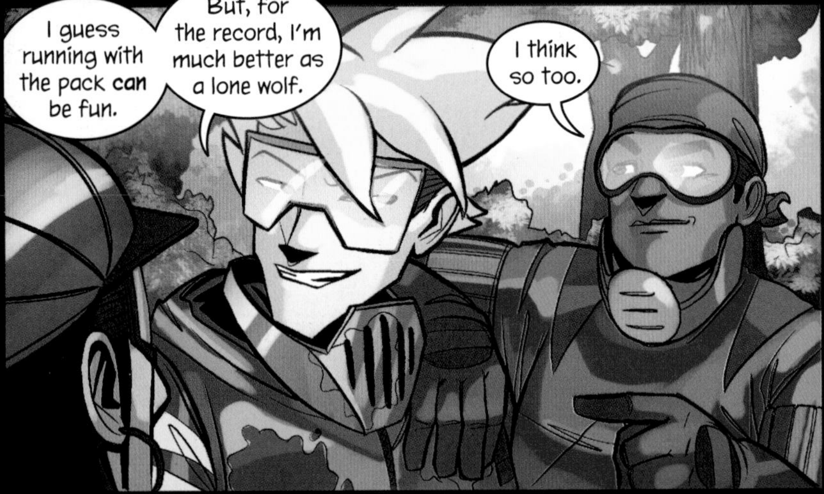
I guess running with the pack **can** be fun.
But, for the record, I'm much better as a lone wolf.
I think so too.

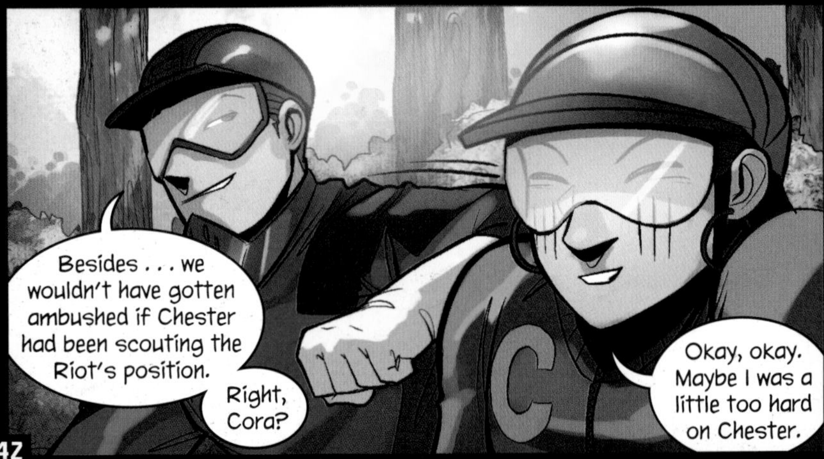
Besides . . . we wouldn't have gotten ambushed if Chester had been scouting the Riot's position.
Right, Cora?
Okay, okay. Maybe I was a little too hard on Chester.

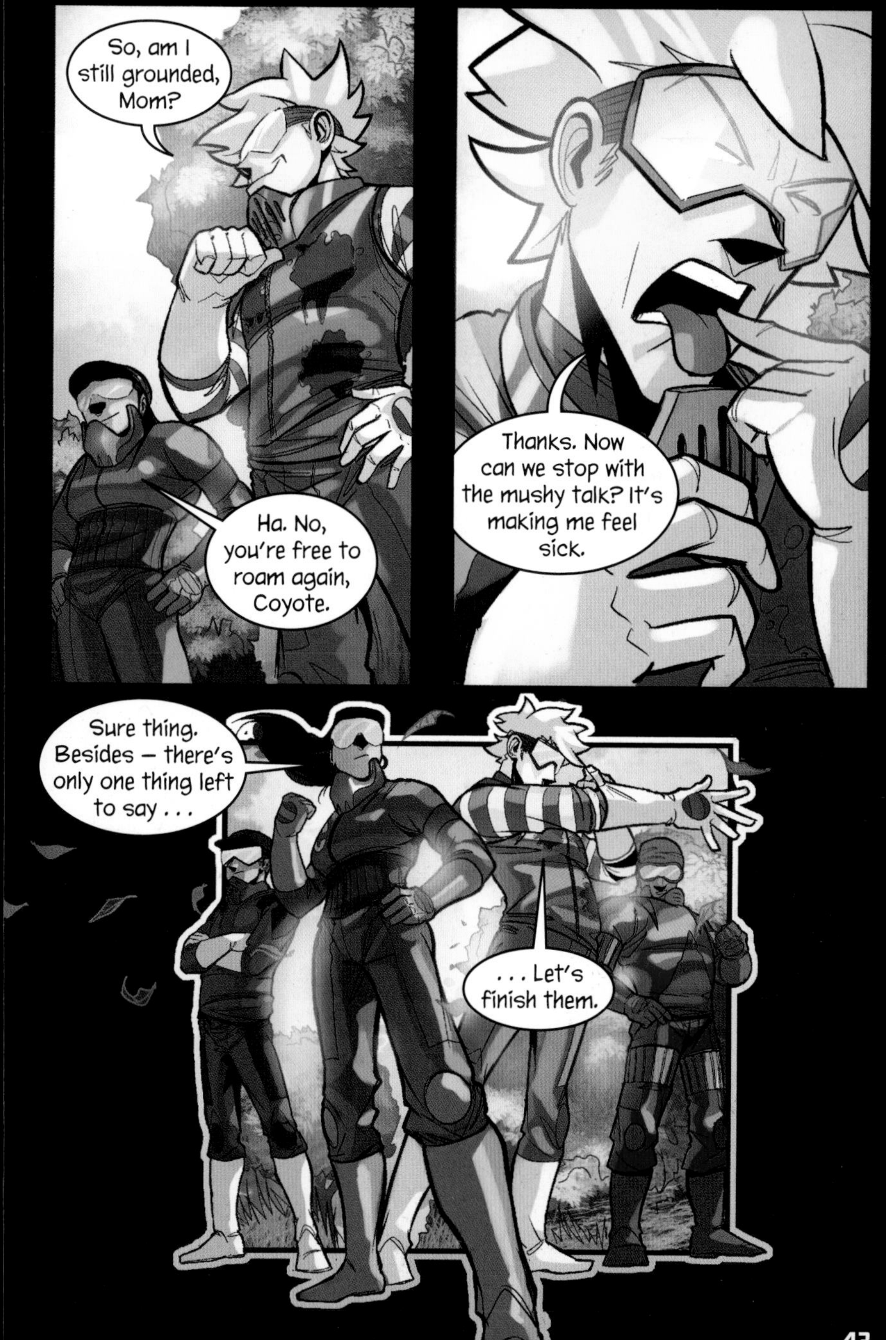
So, am I still grounded, Mom?
Ha. No, you're free to roam again, Coyote.
Thanks. Now can we stop with the mushy talk? It's making me feel sick.
Sure thing. Besides — there's only one thing left to say . . .
. . . Let's finish them.

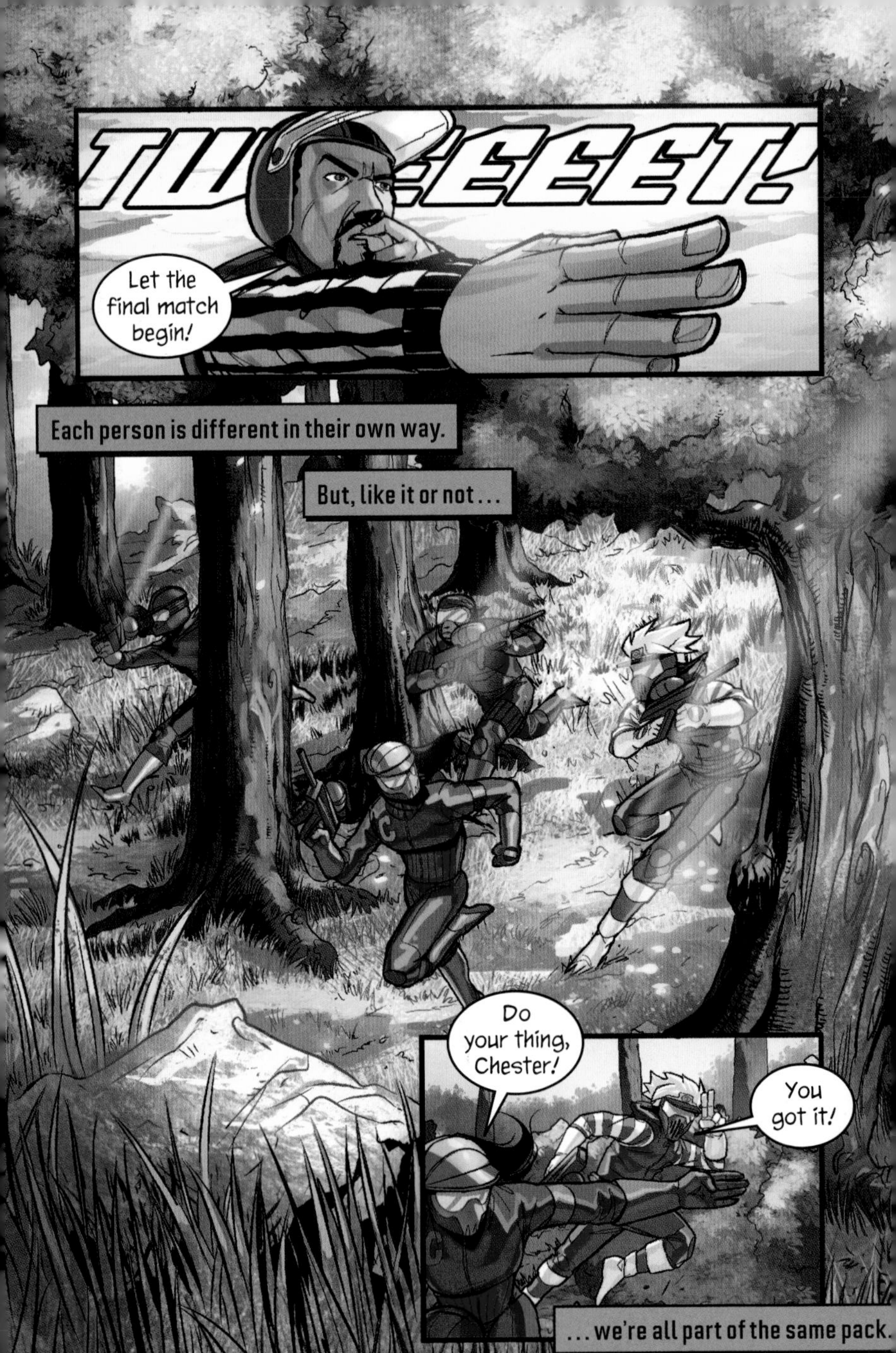
TWEEEET!
Let the final match begin!
Each person is different in their own way.
But, like it or not . . .
Do your thing, Chester!
You got it!
. . . we're all part of the same pack.

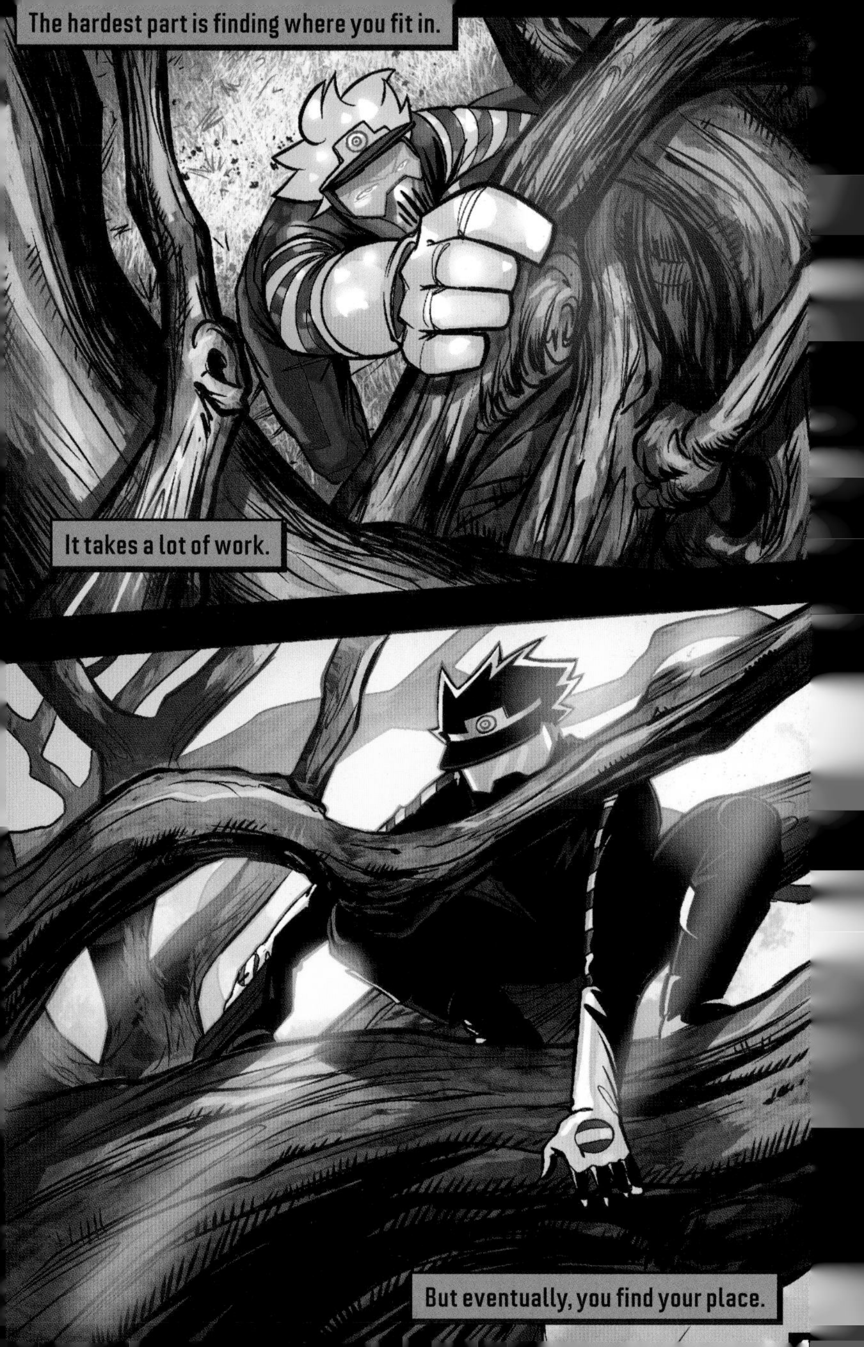
The hardest part is finding where you fit in.
It takes a lot of work.
But eventually, you find your place.

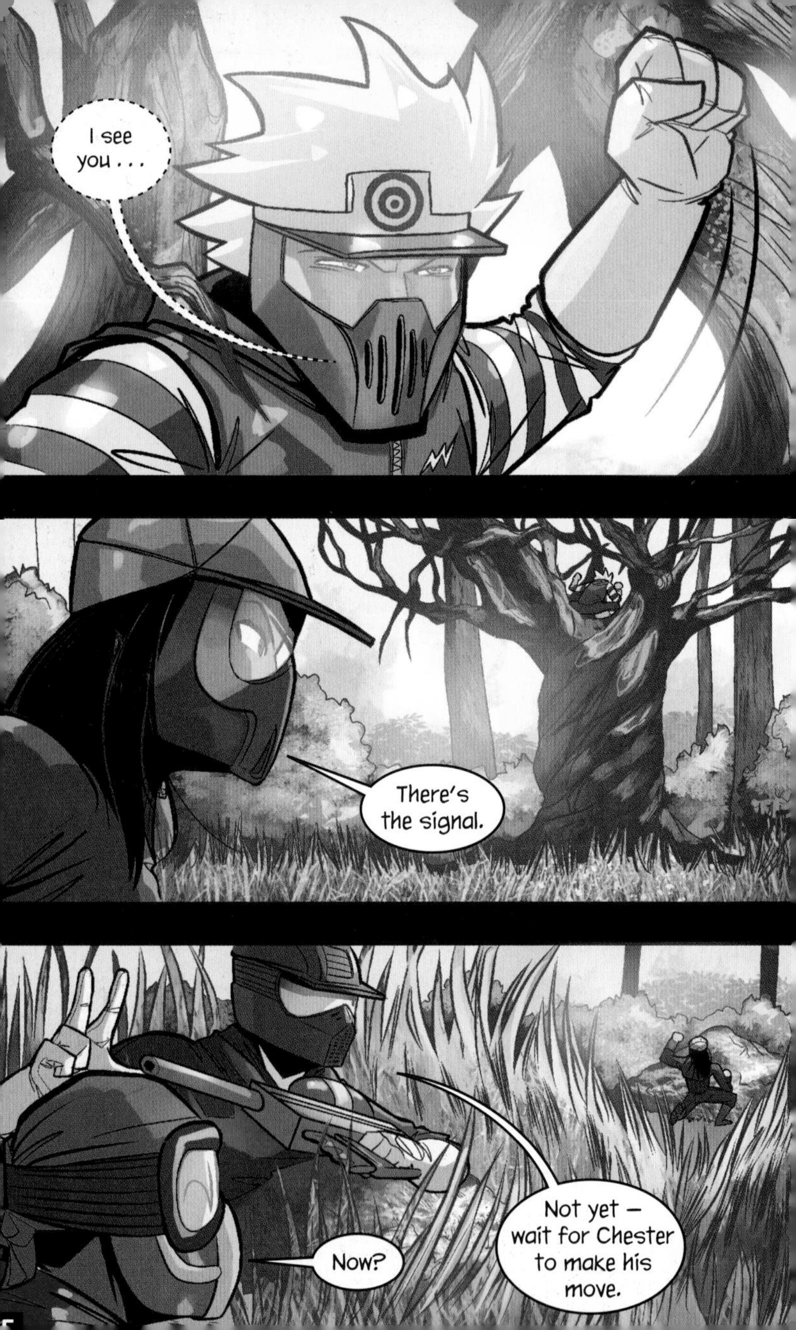
I see you . . .
There's the signal.
Now?
Not yet — wait for Chester to make his move.

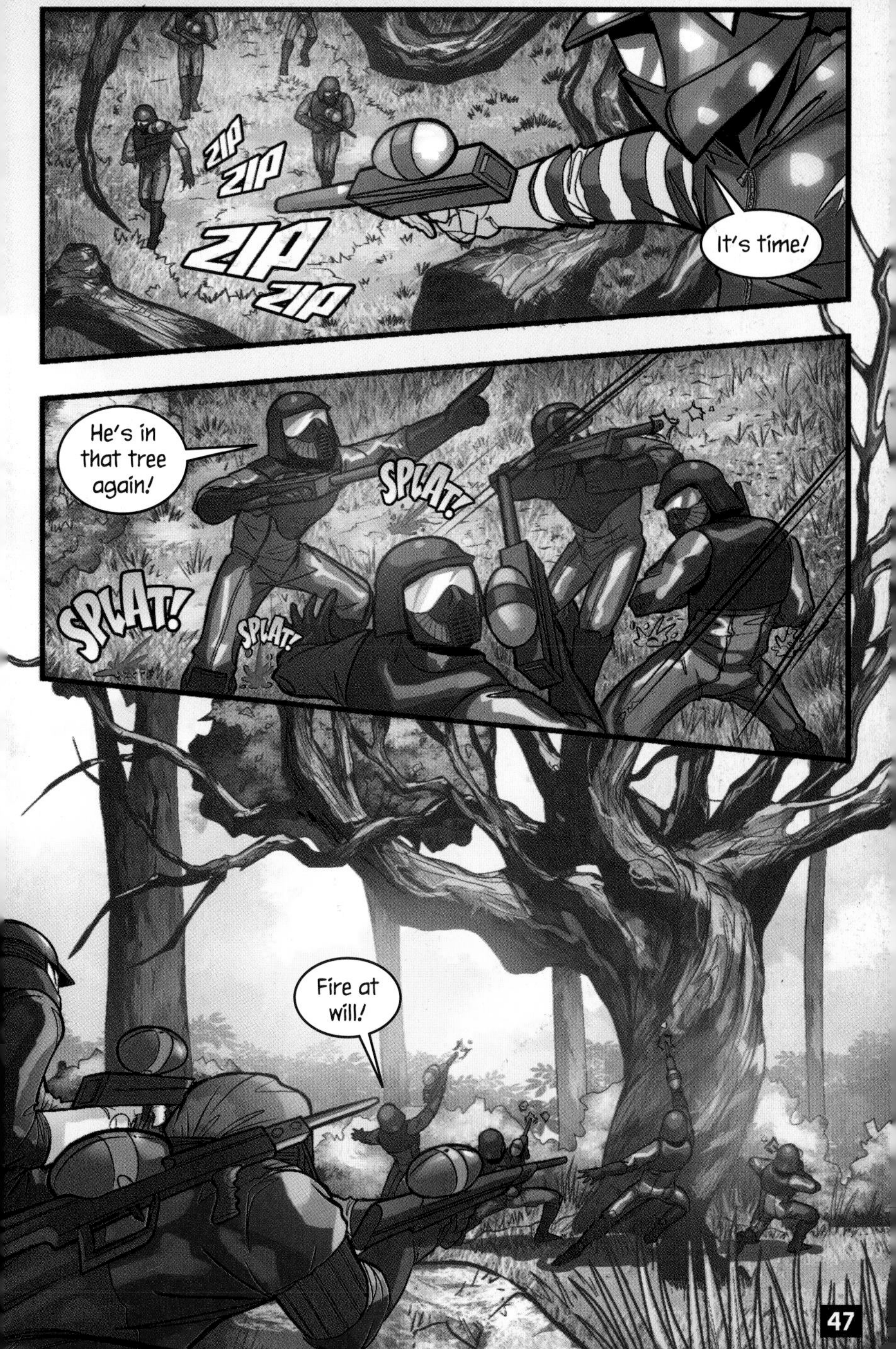
ZIP
ZIP
ZIP
ZIP
It's time!
He's in that tree again!
SPLAT!
SPLAT!
SPLAT!
Fire at will!

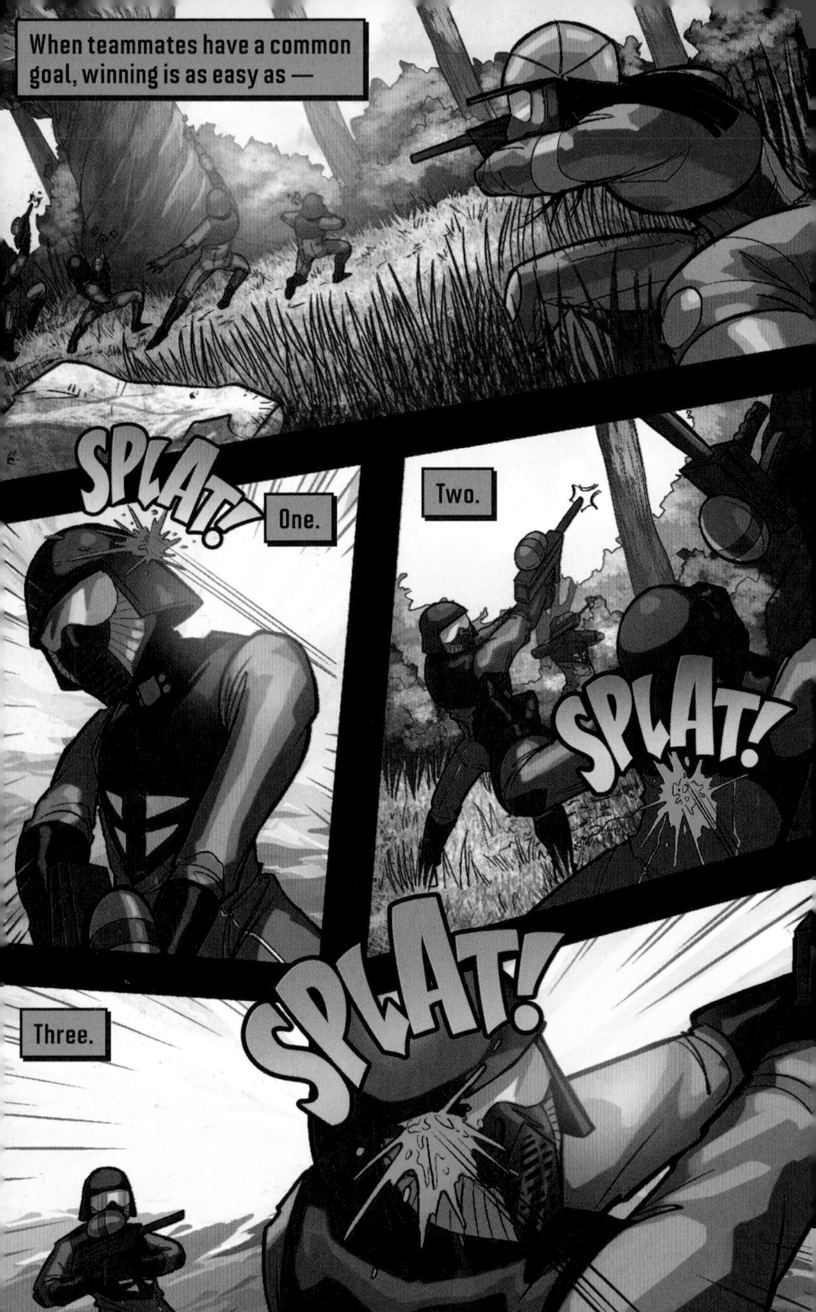
When teammates have a common goal, winning is as easy as —
SPLAT!
One.
Two.
SPLAT!
SPLAT!
Three.

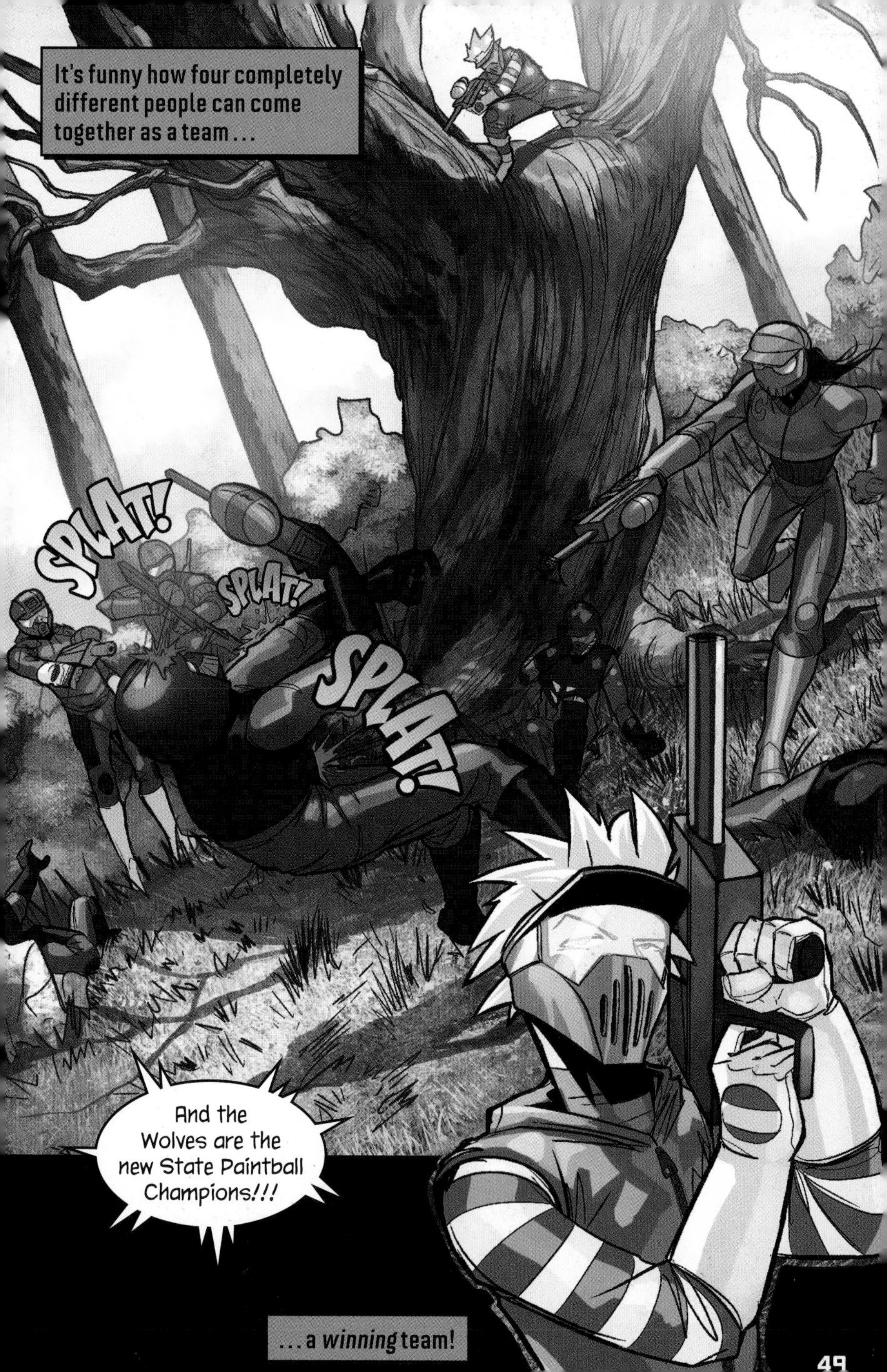
It's funny how four completely different people can come together as a team . . .
SPLAT!
SPLAT!
SPLAT!
And the Wolves are the new State Paintball Champions!!!
. . . a *winning* team!

SPORTS ZONE

STGAME RECAP

NT
TBALL

O
DING

L

L

L

COYOTE

WOLVES

WOLVES TEAM UP TO SUBDUE RIOT!

STORY: After a rocky start, the Wolves regrouped to take down the Riot in the state paintball finals. After accidentally marking his own teammate in the first match, Chester Coyote made up for his mistake by sacrificing himself to save her in the second match. Cora and the other Wolves rallied behind Chester's selfless act to quickly take out the remaining Riot players. It was smooth sailing from there, as the Riot were eliminated two games to one.

Y THE UMBERS

ARKS:
OYOTE: 5
AMIREZ: 6

Sports Illustrated KIDS

UP NEXT: SI KIDS INFO CENTER

BLZ vs BKS 3-1
TGR vs RDR 33-32
EAG vs BAN 14-7
SPA vs WLD 4-3
BAN vs RDR 21-15
RZR vs LIG 4-3
BLZ vs BKS 3-1

SZ POSTGAME EXTRA

WHERE ***YOU*** ANALYZE THE GAME!

Paintball fans got a real treat today when the Wolves one-upped the Riot in the state paintball championship! Let's go ask some fans for their thoughts on the day's exciting matchup . . .

DISCUSSION QUESTION 1

Which member of the Wolves is your favorite — Cora, Chester, Jack, or Peter? Why?

DISCUSSION QUESTION 2

Is it more important to fit in with your friends, or to be yourself? Discuss your answers.

WRITING PROMPT 1

What makes being part of a team fun? What makes it difficult? Do you prefer to do things on your own, or be a part of the team? Write about cooperation.

WRITING PROMPT 2

Imagine that Chester and Cora must compete to decide who will be team captain. Write a story about their competition. What happens? Who wins? You decide.

'WOLVES' BIG WIN SNAPS THE RIOT'S 17-GAME WINNING STREA' SIK TICKER

(AM-bush)—to hide and then attack someone

(KUHV-ur FIRE)—when you fire a paintball marker to distract your opponents and protect your teammates

(FOR-fit)—to be disqualified, or lose, because of a penalty or for doing something wrong

(IN-stingktz)—natural abilities

(KEEN)—sharp or alert

(MARK-ur)—a piece of equipment that fires paintballs

(MARKS-muhn)—someone who has really good aim

(puh-TROLL)—to walk or travel in an area to keep watch on people and scout their positions

(SKOUT)—someone sent to find out and bring back info

(TAK-tiks)—plans or methods to win a game or achieve a goal

EATORS

SEAN TULIEN › Author

Sean Tulien is a children's book editor living and working in Minnesota. In his spare time, he likes to read, eat sushi, exercise outdoors, listen to loud music, and write books like this one. Sean has two scars from his own paintball experiences, but he still loves to play.

ABURTOV › Illustrator

Aburtov is a graphic designer and illustrator who has worked in the comic book industry for more than 11 years. In that time, Aburtov has colored popular characters like Wolverine, Iron Man, Punisher, and Blade. He recently created his own studio called Graphikslava. Aburtov lives with his beloved wife in Monterrey, Mexico, where he enjoys spending time with family and friends.

ANDRES ESPARZA › Inker

Andres Esparza has been a graphic designer, colorist, and illustrator for many different companies and agencies. Andres now works as a full-time artist for Graphikslava studio in Monterrey, Mexico. In his spare time, Andres loves to play basketball, hang out with family and friends, and listen to good music.

FARES MAESE › Colorist

Fares Maese is a graphic designer and illustrator. He has worked as a colorist for Marvel Comics, and as a concept artist for the card and role-playing games Pathfinder and Warhammer. Fares loves spending time playing video games with his Graphikslava comrades, and he's an awesome drum player.

Sports Illustrated KIDS GRAPHIC NOVELS

QUICK COMIC

PETER and NOAH ELLLESTON IN:

POINT-BLANK PAINTBALL

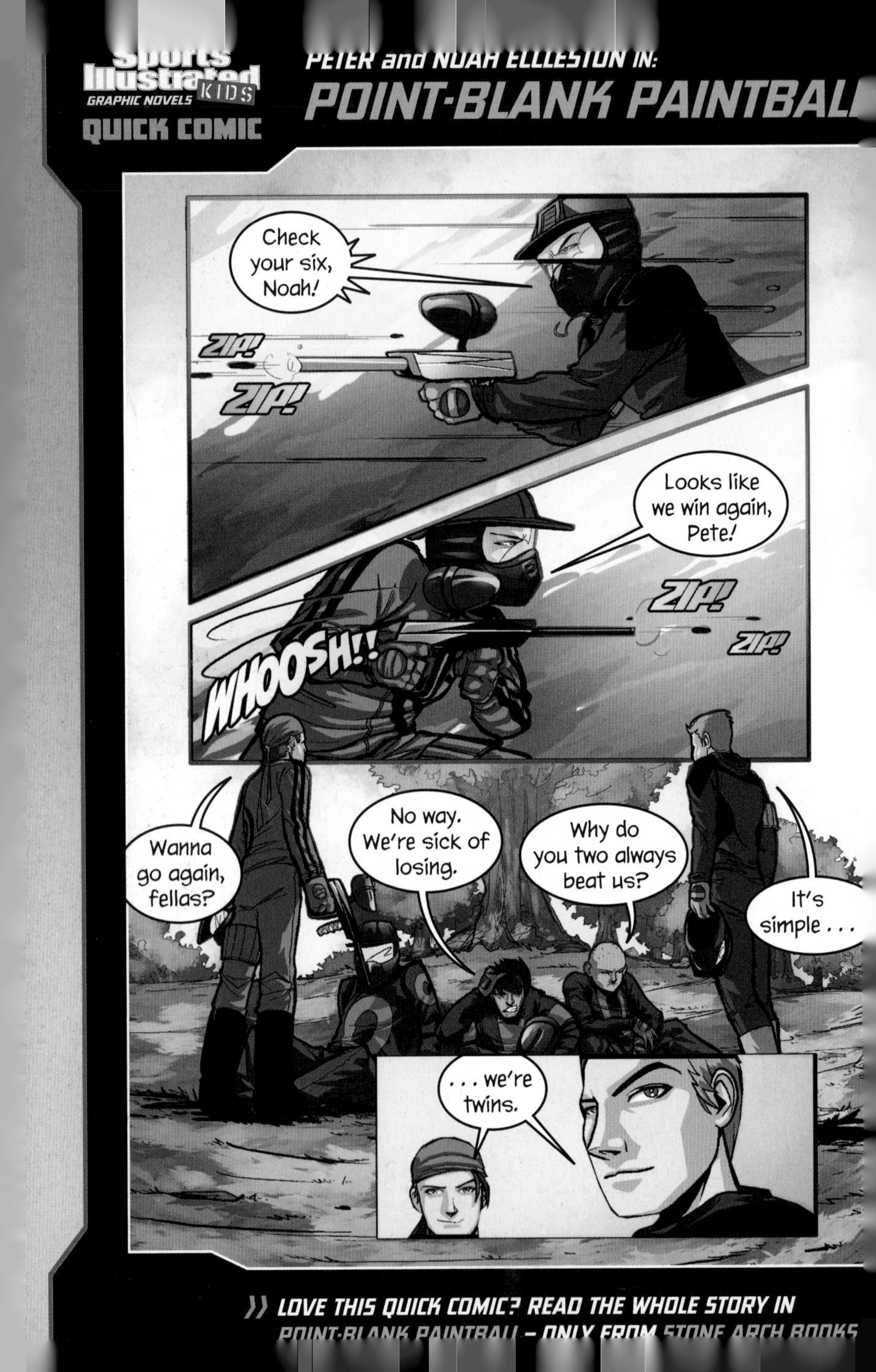
Check your six, Noah!
ZIP!
ZIP!
Looks like we win again, Pete!
ZIP!
ZIP!
WHOOSH!!
Wanna go again, fellas?
No way. We're sick of losing.
Why do you two always beat us?
It's simple . . .
. . . we're twins.

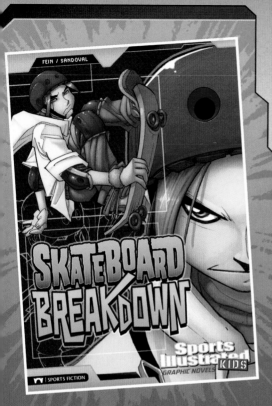

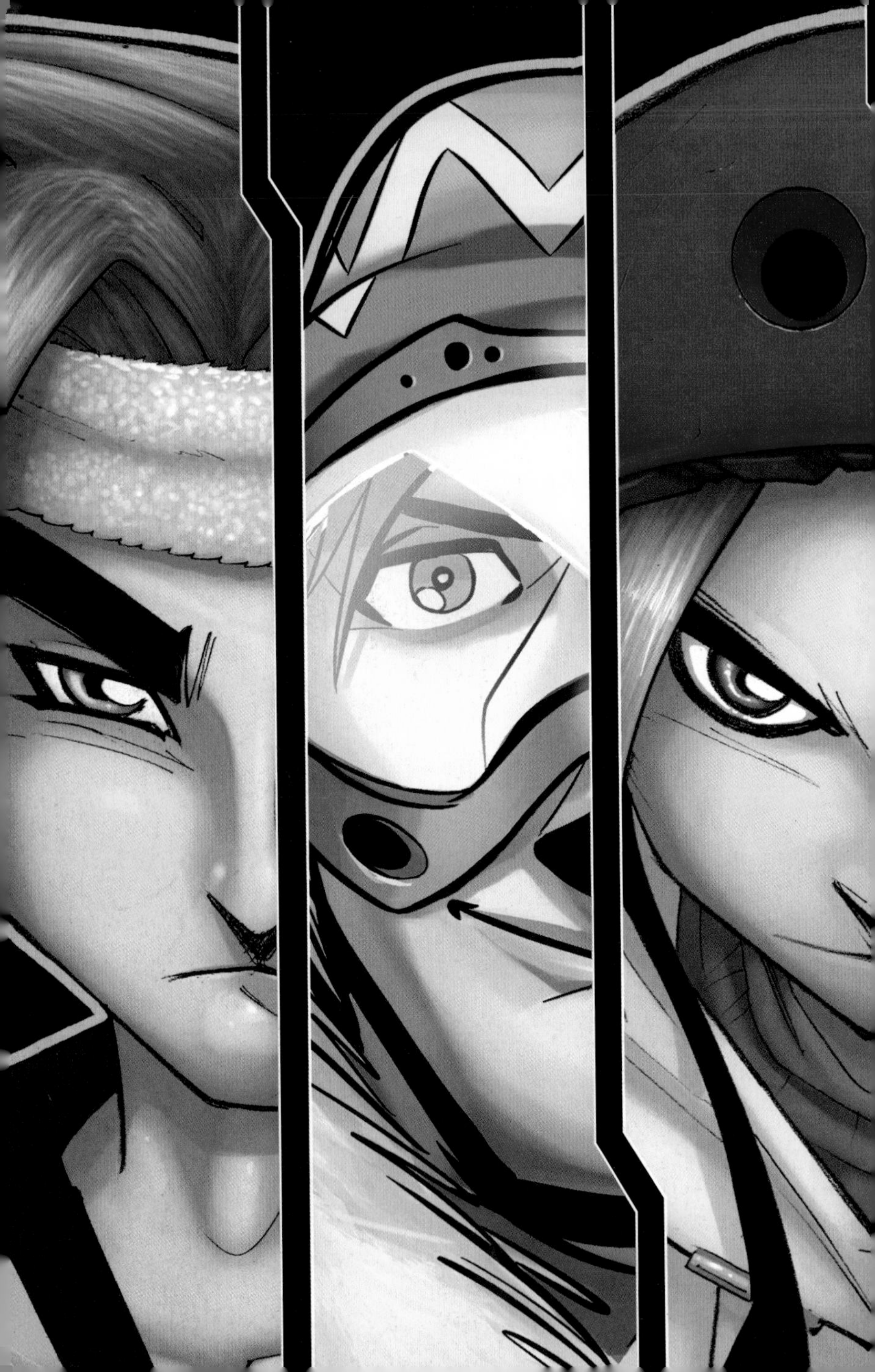

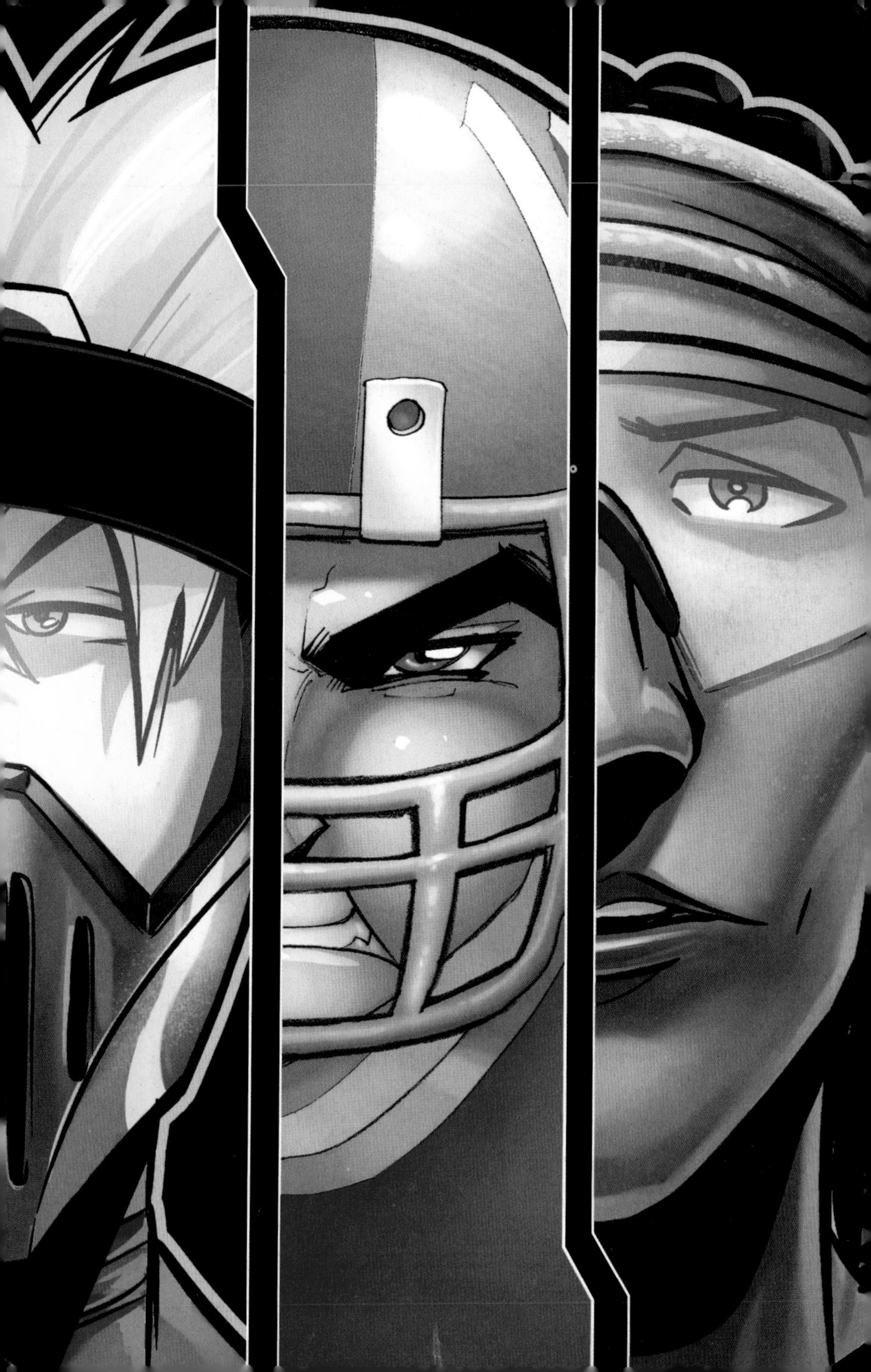

Sports Illustrated KIDS
GRAPHIC NOVELS

STONE ARCH BOOKS
a capstone imprint